Paulie
JOHN INMAN

Dreamspinner Press

Published by
Dreamspinner Press
5032 Capital Circle SW
Suite 2, PMB# 279
Tallahassee, FL 32305-7886
USA
http://www.dreamspinnerpress.com/

Paulie
© 2014 John Inman.

Cover Art
© 2014 Cover photo by DWS Photography.
cerberuspic@gmail.com
Cover design by Paul Richmond.
Cover content is for illustrative purposes only and any person depicted on the cover is a model.

ISBN: 978-1-62798-480-5
Digital ISBN: 978-1-62798-481-2

Printed in the United States of America
First Edition
January 2014

For John B., as always.

Chapter 1

PAULIE BANKS tapped the SEND button and his first novel was gone. Just like that. Off to see the wizard. Or the publisher. Or some flunky at the publishing house who would delete it from existence before it ever *got* to the wizard. Or the publisher.

Paulie was new at this writing business. He didn't know how the system worked. But he did know one thing. With his first completely finished novel under his belt and out there somewhere right this very minute blazing a trail through cyberspace, heading for either fame or ignominy, fated for a quick, merciful death or everlasting fucking life, he could now call himself a writer. He might not be a *published* writer quite yet, but he was still a writer. At least in his own mind.

Paulie sat at his desk in the massive old house he was raised in and listened to the sound of his dog, Hammer, slurping at his balls like a kid slobbering over a Black Cow on a stick. Boy, that dog loved to lick his balls.

Tilting his head to the side to listen harder, and trying to ignore the slurpy sounds of Hammer pleasuring himself, Paulie let the silence of the old house calm him. The sun had set hours ago, and the night was as still as death. No, not death. It was more like the stillness of a... of a... fog bank. Yeah, that was it. Soothing. Deadening. Mindless. Comforting and profound. That was it exactly. The darkness wrapped itself around Paulie like a fog bank rolling in off the ocean. Burying the sea. Burying the land. Burying everything.

And remembering the ocean not two hundred yards from his back door, Paulie suddenly heard the rush and roar of the surf striking the rocks. It was one of those ever-present sounds that loses itself to the ear after a while. Like the ticking of a clock. But Paulie was glad it was always there at his beck and call when he needed it. He loved to hear the surf. It let him know he wasn't alone, that he was part of the world. It was an old friend, the surf. Like a dog. Like Hammer.

And like the gang who would arrive shortly. The people he loved more than any others on the planet. They would soon be wending their way into San Diego, like his novel was wending its way out. On the air. Invisible. Somewhere up in the ether. Strapped in, miles from the ground.

His friends. His crazy friends.

He gave a chuckle of anticipation. *Jesus, I hope I have enough booze on hand.*

Paulie sat at his computer in the library, surrounded by hundreds and hundreds of wonderful old books. At his grandmother's request, Paulie had spent long weeks during his fifteenth summer arranging the books by author. And there they still neatly sat, staring out from the beautiful teak shelves his grandfather had built more than fifty years ago, long before Paulie was ever born or dreamed of.

And as he always did when his grandmother sprang to mind, Paulie held his breath and cocked his head to the side, listening. Listening. For the sound of her cane tapping the hardwood floor somewhere overhead. Or the strains of an aria, from *Aida* or *Carmen* or *Die Fledermaus*, which his grandmother had listened to on the radio as she knit or cooked or simply sat in the sunroom and surveyed her garden—the garden she could, sadly, no longer work herself. No, that job too had fallen to Paulie, her only grandson. With her husband dead and buried for the past thirty years, Paulie had become the one true remaining love in her life. And she had seemed to cherish every moment she spent with him.

Paulie's mother and father were also gone, dead in a car crash when Paulie was four. His grandmother had scooped him into her trembling arms that day, the day her daughter and her daughter's husband had died. She had wept as she pressed her lips to Paulie's hair and told him not to worry, she would care for him. He would always have a home with her. And when she was gone, the house would be his as well. One day it would all be his, she said. Everything.

And just as his grandmother had tearfully predicted, two decades later it all came true.

She had passed away quietly one morning a little over a year ago as she sipped a cup of tea in the sunroom, her favorite room in the house. He was with her on that day, having coffee. They were sharing a little plate of biscuits. Sort of a midmorning snack before he went outside to tackle the cleaning of the koi pool in the back yard. He watched, frozen in dismay, as her kind old face suddenly paled. Her eyes opened wide for a moment in surprise, and she just had time to carefully set her china teacup out of harm's way on the little wicker table beside her chair before her head slumped onto her chest and she closed her eyes forever.

An aneurysm, the doctors said. A wonderful way to go, they also said. Here one second and gone the next. And Paulie supposed he agreed with them. He was glad his grandmother, the kindest, sweetest woman he had ever known, had not suffered in the end. He was glad she had maintained her dignity until the day her eyes finally closed upon the world. And he was glad he was with her when the time came for her to leave. She had loved him very much, and Paulie knew it. She would have wanted him there at the end. And Paulie was glad he could give her that much, even if it was only by a random stroke of luck that he was sitting with her at that fateful moment.

He would always be grateful for that one little blessing of fate.

And grateful for everything his grandmother had done for him. The money. The house. The memories. Paulie was set for life. Financially and emotionally. Well raised, well loved.

And not only had his grandmother been the greatest influence of his young life, she had also been his staunchest supporter in the things he chose to do with that life.

Such as writing.

She read every one of his stories, even the ones printed in pencil in a childish hand when he was eight years old and just beginning to make up tales. She laughed over them and cried over them and praised them to high heaven.

Once, she pulled him close as he stood beside her chair and told him in her crooning, gentle voice, "Don't ever stop writing, Paulie. It's what you were born to do, I think. So don't ever stop. You'll never be happy if you do."

And Paulie *had* never stopped. He majored in English and studied literature and creative writing in college. He read everything he could get his hands on. And he wrote. He turned out story after story, none of which had ever earned him so much as a nickel.

On the day of his grandmother's funeral, after all their friends and neighbors had finally gone, leaving the old mansion with an echoing, sad silence, Paulie spent time in his grandmother's room. Just to say goodbye. While there, he touched her things, each and every one of them triggering a memory. Her necklaces, tidily placed atop her dresser on little racks. Her lace handkerchiefs, neatly folded and stacked in a drawer. Her little prayer book, sitting on the nightstand by the bed.

In a bottom drawer, all by themselves, he found all the stories he had ever written for her, carefully arranged and wrapped in a silk shawl with peacocks on it. They looked well thumbed, as if she had sat alone in her room on many a long, sleepless night, leafing through them, reading those stories over and over and over again.

That thought made Paulie smile even as the tears coursed down his cheeks.

The person who loved him most was gone. Would anyone ever love him that much again? He didn't know. And only time would answer the question.

He folded the stories back inside the lovely silk shawl and carefully stowed the bundle back in the bottom drawer of his grandmother's dresser. Leaving her room, he silently pulled the door closed behind him to give her memories time to be alone. To give her spirit time to adjust to wherever it now resided. But wherever it was, Paulie knew it would be a soothing, genteel place where arias played softly in the background, and the person who loved him more than any other ever had would sit sipping tea and thinking of the boy she had so lovingly raised. She would be watching over him too. He knew that without a doubt. And he would act accordingly. Oh yes. He surely would. To shame her by his actions now would be a betrayal after everything she had done for him. He would never let that happen.

Sitting now, still at his computer in the silent old house, Paulie grinned, remembering his grandmother's reaction to his announcement at the tender age of eighteen that he was gay.

If he expected histrionics at the news, she had disappointed him. She had merely smiled and said, "We are what we are. If you are different, it's because you are special. Don't let anyone tell you differently."

And Paulie's sexual orientation was never mentioned by his grandmother again.

Hammer nudged Paulie's leg, dragging his mind back to the present. Paulie glanced at the clock. It was getting late. Now that he had his master's attention, Hammer pranced around at his feet. It was time for a walk.

Paulie put the computer to sleep and grabbed the leash off the table in the corner, where he had tossed it the last time he used it. He tethered Hammer safely to him—since the dog didn't have enough sense not to simply start running and never look back every time he went outside the door—and together, man and dog set out for their evening constitutional.

Paulie had a million things going through his head as he led Hammer through the La Jolla neighborhood that abutted the grand Pacific, only a stone's throw away.

It was a wealthy neighborhood, and with his grandmother's passing, Paulie was now one of the wealthy residents. And he loved living against the sea. Loved the smell of it. Loved the heat of the sand in the summer and the cold bite of fog in the winter. Loved the lazy, throaty call of the foghorn blasting out from the lighthouse up the coast when the nights were lost in haze. Loved jogging to Cabrillo Point, where the lighthouse stood, and looking out across the water, seeing the whales in the spring, the kayaks and sailboats in the summer, the Navy ships regally sliding in and out of port, one after the other. Day after day after day.

Paulie loved the sea. His grandmother taught him that too.

There were cliffs abutting Paulie's property line, and after a quick tour of the neighborhood, he and Hammer made their way down the wooden staircase that led to the sand and the rocks below. On this night, a full moon hung fat in the sky, lighting his way, and the streetlights up above helped too.

He was not alone as he walked. There were other neighbors, other residents, also taking their pets for an evening walk, and still others, petless, just strolling hand in hand, taking in the night. Some said hello as they passed, some didn't. Paulie always smiled and nodded and tried to keep Hammer from sniffing the occasional leg or humping the occasional Chihuahua, poodle, or mastiff. Being a mutt with the bloodlines of a hundred different breeds coursing through his veins, and all the morals of a serial rapist, Hammer had very eclectic tastes as far as sex went. He would hump anything. It didn't even have to be a dog. Paulie felt a tug on the leash one day and looked back to find Hammer humping a fence post. He even seemed to be enjoying it. There was a crazed look in Hammer's eyes that said, "Damn the splinters! Who cares!"

Poor horny mutt.

There was a well-trod path through the jumbled rocks at the base of the stairs, and then the beach opened up a little farther down. In the moonlight, the sand shone white like alabaster. Ivory breakers lapped at the beach; they too gleamed white in the moonlight as they skimmed and foamed and chuckled in the night.

Looking back up the ragged cliff behind him, Paulie could see the lights of his home shining among the stars behind it. The lights were welcoming. Friendly. With a quiet little thud in his heart, he realized at that moment how much he loved the rambling old house. A mansion, really, if you wanted to get snooty about it.

And while Hammer dug through the sand trying to unearth some poor beast or other, a crab maybe, Paulie, for the millionth time, thought of his grandmother and everything she had done for him. His memories of his parents were so sparse and so incomplete they hardly occupied space in his heart at all. After all, he had barely known them.

But his grandmother was always there. Inside his head. Inside his heart. And as he always did when her face suddenly popped into his thoughts, he cast a silent toast skyward, wishing her well. Letting her know he was happy and suitably taken care of. Just as she had always intended him to be.

Hammer looked up and caught a glimpse of the moon. It seemed to startle him. He plopped his ass in the sand and stretched out his tawny neck, and the next thing Paulie knew, the crazy dog was howling like a wolf. Ahooooo! Ahooooo! A genetic memory of his ancestors must have kicked in, and with him being a mutt, Hammer's ancestors were all over the place. He probably had a shitload of genetic memories to choose from, and at the moment, he picked the noisiest one he could find.

Paulie laughed at the dog's antics, and as soon as Hammer finished howling and decided to poop instead, Paulie plucked a baggie out of his pocket, cleaned up the mess, and headed home with Hammer in tow. A man and his dog. Both happy and content with what life had dealt them.

Paulie had just reached the halfway point on those long wooden stairs up the cliff when another memory burst open inside his head like a water balloon.

A memory of Ben. One of his friends, who would soon be arriving, driving in from Omaha, where he now lived and worked. Ben. Whom Paulie hadn't seen since graduation ceremonies at San Diego State.

Ben. Who was part and parcel of Paulie's all-time favorite memory ever, and who probably, even now, didn't know it.

Ben. His roommate in their last year of college. One of the three best friends Paulie had ever had.

Beautiful Ben.

And as he always did when Paulie's thoughts centered on that one incredible night more than a year earlier—no, wait, almost *two* years earlier—Paulie froze in place. Stunned to immobility by the memory.

Hammer looked up at him, wondering why they'd stopped, but Paulie didn't notice. The dog watched a smile creep across his master's face, bathed as it was in moonlight. And seeing it, Hammer wagged his tail. Only when Hammer figured they had been standing there long enough did he take a tiny nip at his master's shin to get them moving again.

It worked too. Paulie jumped like someone had poked him with a cattle prod. Then he looked down at Hammer and laughed.

"Okay, okay, you bloody mongrel. Let's go home, then."

And home they went.

Not once as they walked did the smile leave Paulie's face. Only now there was a hint of sadness in it.

A hint of—loss.

Ben. Beautiful Ben.

What was now a wonderful memory had once almost killed their friendship completely. And for that, Paulie would never forgive himself.

He and Hammer slowly climbed the long staircase toward the house, and as he climbed—he remembered.

He remembered all of it.

IT WAS a moment of weakness. Or maybe he should blame it on the beer. Whatever it was that caused it, both young men fell into it with very little hesitation or fear of regret.

But regret would indeed come. Later. At least for one of them.

They were an inseparable foursome that last year of college—Paulie, Ben, Jamie, and Trevor. A force unto themselves. Nonjoiners every one. No fraternities sought them out, and none were courted by them, for truthfully, they were perfectly content in each other's company and fanatically focused on their schoolwork. They didn't have time for college politics or grandstanding fraternities. Their driving passions were steered only toward themselves, their friendship, and their educations. Little else mattered.

Through his junior year, Paulie stayed at the La Jolla mansion while he attended San Diego State. However, in one of the few instances of rebellion Paulie could ever remember exerting where his grandmother was concerned, he politely refused to live at home while he attended his final year of college. He needed to be on his own, he patiently told her, but he would come by as often as he could to visit and help her out. She had acquiesced. In fact, she did *more* than acquiesce. Rather than let him go to work at some menial job and possibly impede the progress of his final year of schooling, she set him up with a checking account that would easily pay for his needs while he lived off campus. And for that act of generosity, Paulie loved the woman all the more. Her kindness seemed to have no limit. No boundaries. None at all.

Ben was Paulie's roommate in a tiny two-bedroom apartment just off the campus. Both being English majors, they had met in class and struck up a friendship their freshman year. Paulie wanted to write, and Ben wanted to teach. When their final school year began, they decided to share expenses on a small apartment Ben had found but could not afford on his own. Their apartment building was packed with students—studying, drinking, loving. Jamie and Trevor lived one floor above. All four of the young men were straight-A students. Boisterous, funny, handsome, irreverent.

While Trevor and Jamie had an on-again off-again love affair during that final year, both being proudly and defiantly gay, Paulie and Ben restricted themselves to friendship, which in a perfect world might not have been Paulie's choice at all. Unfortunately for Paulie, Ben was the only straight one in the bunch. He was also the son of a Methodist minister, although it didn't seem to bother Ben knowing his best friends were gay. In fact, he sometimes flirted with either Jamie or Trevor, or both of them together, but it was only in fun and everyone knew it.

Paulie was always a little surprised that Ben never flirted with him. Perhaps because, living together, they were simply too close for that sort of thing. And even Paulie had to admit it would likely get awkward, what with the two of them residing side by side in that tiny apartment with one bathroom and no bedroom doors.

So Paulie acted accordingly. He and Ben were friends, even *close* friends, but he never crossed the line that might twist their perfect friendship into something else. Or destroy it completely.

Ben did not seem to think Paulie was attracted anyway. He oftentimes would stroll around the apartment naked while Paulie sat studying at the old dinette set in the kitchen. When he did, Paulie would watch Ben under lowered lashes, head bent over his books, but it was only a ruse, for he sure as hell wasn't studying. Not while Ben stood naked before him—pouring a glass of milk from the fridge or building a sandwich or simply grabbing a soda. His long, lanky frame was the most beautiful Paulie had ever seen. Veined, furry forearms, nicely defined chest. Hairy legs. A tiny line of dark hair trailed down from his belly button to blossom into a forest of black pubic hair surrounding Ben's luscious uncut cock, which Paulie had never seen erect. But God, he had longed to.

Ben's deep brown eyes were the sort that, had Paulie chosen to put them in writing, he would have unhesitatingly and unabashedly called smoldering. And smoldering they were. Especially when Ben was expounding on a fabulous book he had just read, or a beautiful woman he had just seen. Then there was the way he looked after a long run, his tall frame wrapped in only running shorts, his chest heaving, his shock of black hair soaked in sweat and hanging in his face. His lean strong legs shiny with perspiration and trembling with the exertion of trying to attain a five-minute mile, which he never did.

Sometimes after a run, Ben would shower, then plop himself down, as naked and beautiful as the day he was born, in the chair opposite where Paulie was studying at the kitchen table. It was those times when Paulie was glad there was a tabletop to hide his lower half beneath. Without it, his hunger for Ben would have been blatantly obvious. And embarrassing.

Paulie always made it a point to respect the fact that Ben was off limits, although more than once, Paulie's need to reach out and touch and taste the man was almost unbearable. Just a simple smile from Ben was sometimes enough to make Paulie weak with desire. For Ben had a smile that was a knockout. On more than one night, Paulie had lain in his bed, jacking off to the memory of Ben's heavenly smile.

And it was that smile that finally got Paulie into trouble.

It happened after a particularly wild night of drinking at the Rathskeller by the bay. The four of them were there to celebrate the end of finals and their upcoming graduation on the following day. Needless to say, spirits were high.

It was also on that night that Jamie and Trevor had finally declared their undying love for each other. Perhaps that had had something to do with Paulie finally letting loose and showing his passion for Ben as well.

As they stumbled toward their individual apartments that night, Ben and Paulie watched Jamie and Trevor reel off toward the staircase, wrapped in each other's arms, giggling and flirting before they made it to the floor above, practically having sex before they closed their apartment door behind them. Propriety in public places had never been high on Jamie's or Trevor's list of aspirations. Especially when they were drunk.

Laughing at the two of them staggering off arm in arm and groping each other's asses, Ben and Paulie chuckled their way into their own apartment.

The place was a shambles. With school over and only graduation exercises yet to attend, they were preparing to move. After tomorrow they would be adults, on their own, living in an adult world. Sturdy, conscientious, hard-working, boring adults.

It was kind of a sad realization, which might account for the number of beers they had each consumed at the Rathskeller. And Paulie never had been a very good drinker. In truth, neither had Ben. On this night, they were both just one tiny step away from being positively shitfaced.

And as soon as their apartment door closed behind them, their actions pretty well proved it.

It started innocently enough with Ben trying to unbutton his shirt and failing miserably because of his drunken fingers. Happy to be of assistance, Paulie hiccupped and came to the rescue. Oh wait, maybe *happy* wasn't quite the correct word. Maybe *ecstatic* would be a little closer to the truth.

He had Ben's buttons undone before Ben could kick his shoes off.

As Ben pulled off his shirt, he mumbled, "Sank you."

"Don't mention it." Paulie grinned, his face three inches from Ben's.

And when Ben fumbled around with his belt buckle, Paulie came to the rescue *again*.

"Your fingers aren't working, son. Let me lend you a hand."

Ben started giggling. "By all means. Most kind. Most kind."

Paulie dropped to his knees in front of Ben and placed his hands on Ben's belt buckle. Looking up, he saw Ben gazing down at him with a sexy smile twisting his lips.

That smile got Paulie moving all right. He popped open the belt buckle, flicked the button on Ben's jeans with a simple twist of thumb and forefinger, and grabbing Ben's thigh so he wouldn't lose his balance—*Jesus, I'm drunk*—Paulie slid Ben's zipper down, exposing a crisp sea of white linen: Ben's boxer shorts. The only kind he ever wore.

"Thanks, old man," Ben said. He did a quick shimmy and his trousers slid to the floor, exposing those beautiful long legs Paulie loved to stare at so much when Ben wasn't looking.

Again, Paulie looked up at Ben's face as Ben stepped out of his trousers. He stood now in front of Paulie in nothing but socks and boxers. God, he was beautiful. And he was still looking down at Paulie with that sexy smile and those sexy eyes burning a hole straight into Paulie's brain. Somehow, Ben didn't look quite as drunk as he had before.

Paulie hooked a couple of fingers in the elastic waistband of Ben's boxer shorts and said, rather matter-of-factly, he thought, considering the circumstances, "Guess I'll just finish the job, then, if you don't mind."

"Not at all." Ben grinned. "Do what you will."

So Paulie did. He tugged the boxers down to the floor in one swift motion, and there it was, directly in front of his eyes, that beautiful uncut cock he had glimpsed so many times before and longed to reach out and worship. And now here Paulie squatted with it smack in front of his face. As luck would have it, the darn thing seemed to be begging for a little attention. How fortuitous was that?

Still on his knees, Paulie sucked in a little breath of air, and reaching up, he cupped those heavy dark balls in his fingertips just to feel the weight of them. At his touch, Ben sucked in a breath of air too.

Paulie watched, mesmerized, as Ben's cock stretched itself out, languidly lengthening, pushing itself away from the nest of pubic hair it rested in. It lifted its head, oh so slowly, until it stood proudly erect, inches from Paulie's nose.

A wondrous smile transformed Paulie's face. He looked like a kid on Christmas morning.

Still cupping Ben's balls, Paulie circled that beautiful long cock with his other hand and slid the foreskin back exposing the glans. It was his very first glimpse of that magical kingdom, and Paulie's eyes dimmed in lust just looking at it.

He longed to wrap his lips around it, but again, he looked up at Ben's face. Ben's eyes were closed. His lips parted. As Paulie watched, Ben opened his eyes and gazed down at him. When Ben spoke his voice was husky with desire.

"Rich boy is taking the bull by the horns. Finally."

Paulie's voice was so hoarse from passion, it almost sounded like a croak. "Horn," he said. "Singular. And what a horn it is."

Ben laughed and stepped a little closer. "Then toot that fucker, Paulie. Play me a song."

Paulie smiled and blew a little flurry of wind across the head of Ben's cock. He thought he detected a hint of a shudder in Ben's legs when he did it. And he knew he saw that beautiful cock expand just a little bit more, growing just a little bit fatter and a little more erect.

"Come to the bed," Paulie said. "We'll be more comfortable."

And Ben grinned. "You da' boss."

Paulie heaved himself to his feet and released Ben's cock. Taking his hand instead, Paulie led Ben into the closest bedroom, which happened to be his own, and gently pushed him down onto the bed.

He switched on the lamp on the nightstand and looked down at Ben, lying there on his side, waiting for him. Paulie's heart hammered in his chest. His own cock, as hard as Ben's, ached for release, so Paulie pulled off his clothes as quickly as he could, scared to death Ben would change his mind. But Ben simply watched him with that sexy smile still playing at his mouth.

When Paulie was naked, he made a tactical decision. He sprawled out facing Ben in the opposite direction, crotch to nose, on the off chance that, you know, Ben might take a notion to reciprocate. Paulie would hate for him to have to travel a long way if, you know, he *did* get it into his head to do that. It was called courtesy. At least that's what all those beers were telling Paulie to call it.

He pressed his face to Ben's naked thighs, kissing him there, relishing the scrape of Ben's leg hair against his face, inhaling the scent of Ben's hot skin.

Scooching up toward the head of the bed, he positioned himself directly in front of Ben's cock, and after tilting its stiffness toward him, he again peeled back the foreskin. With his heart going a mile a minute, Paulie slid the glans all the way into his mouth. This time the shudder that ran through Ben's body was clear and unmistakable.

Paulie closed his eyes and savored the feel of that swollen cock sliding between his lips. He slid his tongue over the slit and tasted a drop of precome that suddenly seeped out. It tasted sweet and salty and hot. Paulie longed for more.

Ben folded one strong, hairy leg up out of the way and Paulie sucked at Ben's cock as he stroked those beautiful fat balls. He was rewarded by Ben raising his hips off the bed and pushing his dick even deeper into Paulie's hungry mouth. By this time, Paulie was smiling as he worked at that gorgeous cock, as happy as he had ever been in his life.

And when Paulie felt Ben's arms circle his waist and pull Paulie into him, Paulie thought he had died and gone to heaven. Paulie looked down and saw Ben, his eyes closed, pressing his face into Paulie's stomach, kissing him there, holding him tight as he pumped his cock into Paulie's eager mouth.

Ben's dick was huge now, and Paulie wondered if he was about to come. He was fucking Paulie's face without holding anything back, and Paulie accepted every thrust hungrily.

Paulie gasped when Ben pressed his face against Paulie's engorged cock and kissed him at the base of his shaft. Paulie could feel his balls pressed to Ben's chin, could feel Ben's hot breath blowing across them, making him tremble, just as Ben was now trembling.

Ben's hand came down and gripped the back of Paulie's head as he shoved his cock ever deeper and harder into Paulie's hot mouth. Ben's breath grew ragged, his hips moved more uncontrollably, and suddenly, without warning, Paulie felt Ben's hot come gush across his tongue and splash against the roof of his mouth.

He pulled his mouth away because he wanted to see, he *had* to see, and the moment he did, a torrent of semen shot across his face, his forehead, and all the way into his hair.

Paulie laughed. He had never in his life seen anyone come like that. With such force. In such quantity.

"Suck me," Ben pleaded. "Don't stop." And Paulie again stuffed that heavenly cock into his mouth. He worked at it until the semen ran dry, until Ben's hips stopped shuddering. Paulie swallowed load after load, and even when Ben was drained, he wanted to beg for more.

Paulie's hips were moving now too. He pressed his cock against Ben's cheek as Ben continued to wrap his arms around his waist and hold him close. But Ben would not take him into his mouth, and truthfully, Paulie had not expected him to.

But Paulie cried out when Ben *did* grip Paulie's stiff cock and begin to gently stroke it. Up and down. Over and over. Slowly at first, then more eagerly. Ben's hand was so hot and so tender as it stroked and caressed his dick that Paulie felt his ass tighten as he pushed his balls into Ben's face, and wonder of wonders, Ben kissed him there and did not pull away. The feel of those beautiful lips on his balls made Paulie gasp and plead for more. And more wonder of wonders, Ben gave it to him! Paulie felt Ben's tongue come out and lick his balls, tentatively at first, then with more passion. When Ben once again laid his lips at the base of Paulie's cock as Ben pumped away at it, Paulie found himself trembling like a madman.

And that was all it took. His come shot out like a geyser, jet after jet, splashing his stomach, his chest. And as it spurted, Ben gently wrapped his fist around Paulie's glans, letting Paulie fuck into it. And Paulie did, humping for all he was worth. Ben's come-soaked fist felt like heaven. Paulie pumped it until he could pump no more.

He finally fell back on the bed, replete, spent. Once again he rolled toward Ben and took Ben's softening cock into his mouth.

And in that position they fell asleep. Or more accurately, passed out.

When Paulie awoke, hours later, he was alone. He could hear Ben snoring in his room.

Paulie lay awake until early morning, thinking about what had just happened. With a smile still on his face, he fell asleep again just as dawn broke over the city. Later, when he awoke for the second time, with the sun high in the sky and the birds singing in the trees outside, Ben was gone.

Aside from a note of condolence Ben had sent on the death of Paulie's grandmother, Ben had not communicated with Paulie again until he responded to Paulie's invitation to visit almost two years later. Both those communications were by mail.

They had not *spoken* since that night.

Chapter 2

THE HOT morning sun blasted golden California sunshine up and down the coast, rather like a trigger-happy kid with a Super Soaker, spraying everything in sight. And while the world was waking up under that heavenly deluge of heat and light, Paulie showered and prepared for the day. Tomorrow his guests would arrive, and Paulie had a million things to do.

The Colonial mansion his grandmother had left him—lock, stock, and barrel—was huge. It covered 4800 square feet, or so an eager-beaver Realtor had once told him after she spent the day measuring and salivating her way around the joint because Paulie needed an estimate on the property's worth for his taxes. The place sat on two lots and was much bigger than Paulie needed, the Realtor finally told him, as if he didn't know it already. After conspiratorially draping her arm around his shoulder like she was his new best friend, she whispered into his ear her appraisal of five million smackers, give or take a few hundred grand, depending on the eagerness of the buyer. The woman obviously had an eye toward selling the property for Paulie and raking in a bigass commission for herself.

But Paulie loved the place, and more importantly, his grandmother had loved the place, so Paulie never once considered selling. When Paulie told the woman as much, she looked like Paulie had just run over her dog with his Lamborghini. Which, by the way, Paulie didn't own. He drove a Ford. And it wasn't even new.

The mansion contained a formal dining room, as well as an eat-in kitchen, a library (which also served as Paulie's writing space), a comfortable living room, a TV room, a less than comfortable formal parlor or receiving room, as his grandmother always called it, a sunroom in the back with beautiful, floral-cushioned wicker furniture and windowed walls and ceiling, and five bedrooms on the second floor, each with a full bath and walk-in closets lined in cedar. The house also boasted six fireplaces, hardwood floors, bay windows at the back and sides, a balcony opening up from Paulie's bedroom on the second floor that overlooked the back patio, and farther out, the grand Pacific Ocean. Paulie's bedroom also overlooked a gigantic back lawn with fruit trees, two fountains, a koi pool, and a stand of Leyland Cypresses in the southeast corner. Tucked in among the cypresses were stone benches, two bird baths, and a couple of huge hammocks, which made for a very nice spot to lounge around in when one needed to get away from one's fucking wealth for a little while, which wasn't often.

Through the french doors exiting the dining room at the back of the property, one could find the vast patio with a grill and picnic tables. Just past the patio, at the bottom of a short flight of brick steps with long, easy risers, sat a kidney-shaped swimming pool, shimmering in the California heat. Behind the pool stood a stuccoed cabana with a wet bar, another TV room with a pool table, and a sauna.

Since it was usually just Paulie and Hammer rattling around the place, most of the second floor, except for Paulie's bedroom at the head of the stairs, was normally closed off, as well as the formal dining room and formal parlor. For the next couple of weeks, however, it would all be opened up for the enjoyment of his guests.

Paulie wasn't trying to show the place off. All of his friends had already visited the mansion on numerous occasions when they were in college and his grandmother was still alive. She told Paulie once that she loved having his friends there. It was nice to hear laughter bouncing off the walls again. And when the four of them got together, a whole lot of laughter was pretty much guaranteed.

When his grandmother passed away a year earlier, his friends had all sent flowers and cards, even Ben. And hearing from Ben for the first time since graduation had almost made the whole horrible experience of burying his grandmother bearable.

It was that opening communication from Ben that prompted Paulie to invite him to the house, along with Jamie and Trevor, for two weeks in July. Even so, Paulie had not expected Ben to accept the invitation. But amazingly, he had. By return post. Paulie had still not actually *spoken* to Ben since the night of their—indiscretion. Even at the graduation ceremony, he had only spotted Ben at a distance. If Jamie and Trevor were curious as to why Ben kept to himself that day, their curiosity was tempered by the excitement of graduating from college and starting a life together, having sworn undying fealty to each other forever.

Their undying fealty, it should be noted, had lasted a grand total of three months. Paulie still wasn't exactly sure what had caused the relationship to implode—and figured it was none of his business anyway. Although he was dying to know.

The thought had even crossed his mind he might worm the truth out of one or both of them on this little vacation he had planned for everyone. But the reason for Jamie and Trevor's breakup wasn't the only thing he would like to clear up when his friends arrived.

First and foremost was the matter of himself and Ben. And the resurrection of their friendship.

Was Paulie nervous about seeing Ben up close and personal again for the first time since that horrible, wonderful night? Hell yes. Oh *hell* yes. But he was equally eager to see the rest of his friends. It would be great to have the gang back together again. Paulie was growing a bit lonely meandering around his vast La Jolla mansion with just Hammer at his side.

At the moment, however, Paulie was too busy to be lonely. He was going batshit trying to get everything ready for his friends' arrival. For it was not only three people coming in the next day to occupy his house for two weeks. It was five. Jamie and Trevor might no longer be together, but they had both taken new lovers, whom Paulie had never met, and those new lovers would be arriving with them. And furthermore, Paulie knew neither Jamie nor Trevor had met his ex's new partner either.

Paulie wondered if there might not be a few snarky displays of fireworks in store when they finally did all find themselves under the same roof. Jamie and Trevor were not exactly the reticent types when it came to partying. At least they hadn't been in college, and frankly, Paulie didn't imagine they had acquired much common sense in the meantime.

Trevor owned a bookstore in San Francisco in the Castro district. Jamie was a banker. Paulie had no idea if they saw each other socially, or if their breakup had ended their friendship completely. Paulie could have asked, he supposed, but he didn't really think it was any of his business. Besides, after two weeks of them all living under the same roof, and considering their propensity for imbibing like drunken sots when they all got together, Paulie knew he would soon learn everything there was to learn. And more.

And then there was Ben.

As far as Paulie knew, Ben was still alone, teaching high school English in Omaha, Nebraska. He had made his dream of being a teacher a reality, and for that Paulie was happy for him. He was only sorry it had to be so far away. Apparently, no woman had been lucky enough to snag the handsome bastard yet. For some reason, that knowledge made Paulie's heart give a happy little patter of hope. Hope for what, he wasn't sure. But hope, nevertheless.

He was anxious to see all of his friends of course. But he was more than anxious to see Ben.

Way more than anxious.

A cleaning crew had been swarming all over the house for three days to get the place in order, dusting, scrubbing, cleaning windows, airing out the rugs and drapery, changing all the linens on the beds. Fresh flowers had been placed here and there to make the joint more cheerful, and Paulie had even hired a caterer to deliver evening meals every day while his guests were in town. He figured his friends could forage for themselves during breakfasts and lunches. As long as the beer cooler and the liquor cabinet were well stocked, they shouldn't have any problems at all.

Yep. It was going to be fun.

PAULIE ENJOYED doing the yard work himself. In fact, he had been doing the yard work since high school, at first to earn extra money from his grandmother, and now simply because he liked doing it. Today he mowed, edged, weeded, laid some new mulch around the Cypress trees in the back, cleaned and filled the birdbaths, and scooped a few leaves off the surface of the pool and the koi pond. He made sure the cabana was stocked with booze, the fridge there filled with plenty of ice and beer, and when he was finished with that, he hosed a pile of dog poop off the sidewalk.

"Damn you, Hammer!"

Hammer just grinned and took off after a butterfly. Dumb mutt.

Paulie stood on the back patio, looking over the property, checking out everything he had just done. The place looked great. Inside and out. He glanced at his watch. It was going onto three in the afternoon. He had been working all day and was just about worn out. Time to clean up and relax with a beer by the pool.

Then he remembered: he had a date—of sorts. The young man was supposed to be here at four. Good Lord, he'd almost forgotten.

Fully expecting to take a shitload of ribbing over the matter, Paulie had also hired a houseboy to attend to everyone's needs— everyone's *domestic* needs, that is—after his guests arrived. The houseboy would live in for the next two weeks and be there every minute of every day to make sure things went smoothly. Paulie was paying handsomely for this little dash of snootiness, but he figured it would be worth it not to have to worry about every tiny thing himself.

He had informed the lady at the employment exchange exactly what he wanted. Someone easy on the eyes, efficient, male, and not afraid of a few drunken homosexuals. And if he could scramble a couple of eggs or maybe flip an omelet, that would be a nice plus. The woman had tittered into the phone and promised to do her best.

Paulie had given the woman the combination to the keypad lock on the front gate so the new houseboy could gain access to the property and signed off with a cheery good-bye.

As he shaved and dried his hair, Paulie wondered what the young man would look like. Not that it mattered, of course. Well, yes it did. And he chuckled at that thought. It might just matter a great deal.

Fresh from the shower, he stood in front of the mirror in the master bath and studied his naked, six-foot-tall reflection in the foggy glass. He studied himself with a critical eye, too, as most young gay men are prone to do. Happily, he could report he didn't look bad at all. Pretty damn nice, actually, if he said so himself.

He wore his wavy blond hair a little longer on top than was the style, but it was neatly trimmed over the ears and at the back of the neck. His face was handsome enough, he supposed. Blue eyes, nice smiley mouth, good teeth. And the rest of the package was acceptable as well, all of it nicely tanned from long hours by the pool, except for a tiny strip of pale flesh across his slim hips and ass where his bathing suit generally clung. Broad shoulders, pretty good pecs, no rippling abs, but no flab either. There was a smattering of blond hair across his chest and a trail of blond hair that dribbled down his torso, over his stomach, past his navel, and into his pubes. The pubes were blond as well. Mousey blond, actually—the darkest hair on his body. His pecker was a reasonably respectable six inches when all fired up and ready to go. (He had measured it once when he was sixteen.) It was neatly cut, heavily veined, and friendly to a fault.

Heading farther south, Paulie's legs were strong, lean, and pelted with blond fuzz, his calves sharply muscled from jogging every other day, the quads nicely delineated. His feet were size thirteen. Gigantic fuckers. One of his big toenails had fallen off a few days ago. A runner's curse. It was kind of embarrassing, but there wasn't much he could do about it. At least it didn't hurt, so it didn't impede his jogging.

Over all, as Paulie studied his naked self in the mirror, he figured he didn't have too much to worry about in the looks department. However, that didn't exactly explain why he didn't have a lover, or even a boyfriend, now he had reached the ripe old age of twenty-four, did it?

While Paulie was still standing naked in the bathroom admiring himself like a twit, the new houseboy rang Paulie's front doorbell at four o'clock on the button, passing the promptness test right off the bat. Which was more than could be said for Paulie.

Since the doorbell rarely rang, what with the locked front gate keeping all the riffraffy peons from wandering in off the street and ringing the laird's doorbell just for shits and giggles, Hammer went nuts, yammering through the mansion like UPS had just unleashed a truckload of cats in the parlor.

Paulie screamed for the mutt to shut the hell up as he yanked his bathrobe off the back of the bathroom door and headed out on the two-mile trek to the front door. At times like this, he really hated having a big house. But the idea of hiring a stuffy old butler to answer the door for him seemed elitist and just plain lazy. A young, sexy houseboy—

well, now, that was a horse of a different color. Yes indeedy. There were all sorts of uses to be found for a young, sexy houseboy.

And here Paulie was, just about to meet his very own. To say his imagination was running wild would have been a vast understatement of the facts.

God, he was a slut.

Making sure all his private bits were properly tucked away beneath his bathrobe and out of public view, Paulie eagerly opened the door to see what the agency had sent him.

As soon as he spotted what was waiting for him on the front step, Paulie made a mental note to send the lady at the employment exchange a fucking bouquet of roses. She had outdone herself. His new houseboy was *gorgeous*.

Tall and handsome and lean like a runner, the young man stood on Paulie's doorstep with a broad smile beaming across his face. His skin was the color of lightly creamed coffee. His hair was buzzed short and he wore a tiny gold ring in his left ear lobe, like Othello.

Apparently misconstruing the look of surprise on Paulie's face, the young man's smile faltered a bit. His luscious dark eyes narrowed just a fraction of an inch.

"Yep," he said. "I'm black."

Paulie blinked. "What?"

"I said I'm black."

Paulie laughed and stuck out his hand. "And I'm white. It's a pleasure to meet you."

With that, the young man's smile slowly ratcheted up to its former glory. It was all Paulie could do not to comment on how beautiful his teeth were. They were scrumptious.

The young man reached out and grasped Paulie's hand. "Sorry. Sometimes it seems to make a difference. You know. Being black."

"You're kidding," Paulie said.

"Nope."

Glancing down at the guy's massive paw encircling his, Paulie was amazed by the size of the thing. It was without a doubt the biggest hand he'd ever seen. Paulie wondered if *all* the man's appendages were that big.

He tried to push that thought away before it got him into trouble. He was, after all, standing here naked except for the flimsy bathrobe he'd wrapped around himself. He wouldn't want any of his own appendages popping up and making a nuisance of themselves. Didn't think he'd want to be explaining *that* to the woman at the agency.

"In that case," Paulie said, "let me be the first to apologize for all the assholes in the world."

At that, the young man laughed—a deep, throaty chuckle that made Paulie grin. Through his electrifying smile, he said, "I've been wondering when somebody would."

Still gripping his hand, Paulie said, "I'm Paul. Paulie, if you prefer."

"I'm Jeff. And no, it isn't short for Jefferson."

"So it's Jeffrey, then."

"Yeah. Jeffrey. Jeffrey Wallace."

"Well, Mr. Jeffrey Wallace, come on inside. And stop being so defensive."

"Am I being defensive?"

Paulie snickered and tugged him through the door. "Just a little."

In the foyer, Jeffrey took a moment to look around. He seemed impressed.

Then he looked down with considerable alarm. Hammer had come out of nowhere and clamped his front legs around his shin. The dog was holding on for all he was worth as he humped away at Jeffrey's calf muscle like crazy. Jeffrey could feel the dog's pecker trying to find an orifice to bury itself in. And good luck with that.

"Uhhh—friendly dog."

Paulie jumped when he saw what Jeffrey was looking at. "Oh crap! Hammer, stop that!"

Hammer didn't look too happy about it, but he did stop. He stalked off, still humping the empty air. Paulie couldn't really blame him for jumping the guy. Jeffrey Wallace was imminently jumpable. But still—the least you should do is ask first.

Once the excitement was over, Paulie gave his feet a shuffle and looked embarrassed. "Um, did the lady at the agency tell you what I wanted? Did she tell you who you'd be, uh, working for? I mean with. I mean among."

"You mean besides a horny-ass dog?"

Paulie blushed. "Yeah. Besides that."

Paulie looked up at Jeffrey looking down at him. The man was really tall. Maybe six six. Paulie felt a little like a tiny moon being sucked into the guy's orbit. Damn, he was handsome.

"You mean a houseful of gay guys?" Jeffrey asked. "Yeah, she told me. I'm a gay guy too, so it shouldn't be a problem. Unless, of course, some of your houseguests belong to that fraternity of assholes you were talking about earlier."

"Uhh, no. I don't think so."

"That's a relief."

"Golly, you don't look gay" was all Paulie could think to say.

"Well, good," Jeffrey said. "You kinda do."

He laughed at the surprised look on Paulie's face.

"That was a joke," Jeffrey said.

"No, it wasn't."

Jeffrey shrugged, but he was smiling while he did it. "Well, maybe not entirely."

"I think we're going to get along just fine," Paulie said, his own face beaming now.

Jeffrey grinned. "So do I."

"Then follow me. Before we start, I'll show you to your room."

"Servant's quarters?"

"No. Upstairs with the white folks."

"I don't have to lie under the covers at the foot of the master's bed and warm his feet, do I?"

"Not unless you want to. And yeah, I saw that movie too."

They laughed *again*. This was going better than Paulie had ever imagined it would.

Trailing Paulie up the stairs, watching Paulie's bare calves beneath the hem of his robe, climbing in front of him, Jeffrey licked his lips and said, "This is going to be fun."

To which Paulie answered, "Yeah, I'm kind of getting that vibe as well." He didn't mention it, but the fun vibe wasn't the *only* vibe he was getting. Paulie didn't know it, but that wasn't the only vibe Jeffrey was getting either.

They reached the second floor. "You're at the other end of the hall."

"Is that like the back of the bus?"

"Maybe. But it's a really nice bus."

Jeffrey looked around at the paintings on the wall and the brocaded carpet on the hallway floor and the little glimpse of a swimming pool he saw through a window as they passed. "Nice bus indeed," he mumbled to himself.

To make conversation, Jeffrey said, "In case you're wondering, I'm not a butler in training or anything. I'm working my way through college. Beaumont University."

"Wow," Paulie said, impressed. "Expensive school."

"I know. Thank God for scholarships."

"You got a scholarship at Beaumont?"

"Yeah."

"Wow," Paulie said again, even more impressed than he was before. Beaumont was one of the toughest schools in the country. He ushered Jeffrey through the last door on the right. "Studying what?"

"Biology."

"Holy fucking shit! No kidding?"

"No kidding."

"Well, I must say, it's quite a coincidence," Paulie said.

"Why's that? Were you a biology major?"

"No, but I flunked it in high school."

Jeffrey laughed. "Well, there you go. Small world."

Jeffrey scanned the room. Jesus, he'd never slept in a place this fancy in his life. It even had a canopied bed. "Am I paying you, or are you paying me?"

"I'm paying you. And while you're here, I don't want you to feel like a servant. I would appreciate it if you *acted* like one around the guests but you really don't have to *feel* like one. That make sense?"

Jeffrey nodded. He seemed sincerely touched by the friendly overture. "Yes. It does. Thank you. I won't disappoint you. I'll be the best little houseboy you've ever had."

"Not that there's anything little about you," Paulie said, again eyeing the man from top to bottom.

Jeffrey gave him a secretive smile, and said, "You got that right."

Paulie felt a rush of heat climbing up the back of his neck. What the hell was that all about? As if he didn't know.

"I assume you have a car out there somewhere on the street. You can bring it in and park it on the drive at the side of the house if you like. The agency lady said you would bring everything with you you'd need for a two-week stay, so I'll give you some time to bring it in and stow it in the room before I show you around and acclimate you to your duties. That be okay?"

Jeffrey stuck out his hand. "That's wonderful. Thank you, Paul."

"Paulie, actually. That's what everyone calls me."

"Paulie it is, then. At least when we're alone. Among the partakers of your hospitality, I'll call you 'Sir.'"

Paulie smiled. "Thank you. And I'll call you Jeffrey. That work for you?"

"Works just fine."

After a friendly but awkward moment, during which they both realized how much they liked each other, Jeffrey said, "I'll just go get my stuff then, Paulie. Be right back."

And Paulie watched him go before heading off down the hall to his own room to get dressed.

He figured he'd been naked around the man long enough.

Well. Maybe not *quite* long enough.

Jesus, the guy was hot! He should hire people more often.

PAULIE WAS lying on an inflatable raft in the middle of the pool and sucking on a beer while he bobbed there in the water, winding down from his day's exertions. Way off inside the house, he could hear Jeffrey humming a song in his deep baritone voice as he stowed his belongings in the bedroom at the end of the second floor hallway—his new digs for the next two weeks. To Paulie's astonishment, the humming was remarkably on key. And astonishing Paulie even more, the tune was an aria from *Rigoletto*. "La Donna è Mobile." Paulie remembered it as one of his grandmother's favorite arias.

Paulie was slightly amazed that Jeffrey would know the song. Then he berated himself for thinking it. The guy was a biology major, for Christ's sake. He probably had all kinds of hidden skills and talents and interests and accomplishments Paulie didn't know about, not to mention an IQ that hovered around the stratosphere. Biology majors aren't exactly morons, after all. And it wasn't because Jeffrey was black that Paulie was surprised he knew opera. It was because he was young. Paulie had attended many an opera at his grandmother's behest, and frankly speaking, the number of opera-goers Paulie had spotted under the age of eighty was pretty damn slim.

Paulie looked over at Hammer. He was floating a couple of feet away, lying atop a smaller inflatable raft, chewing on a plastic giraffe. His favorite toy. When Hammer spotted Paulie looking at him, he lifted his head, dropped his ears, and looked guilty.

"You peed in the water, didn't you?" Paulie asked.

But Hammer refused to answer. He just went back to gnawing on his giraffe. In Hammer's mind, discretion was obviously the better part of valor.

"You sink a tooth in that raft," Paulie said, "and you'll be swimming home."

Hammer ignored that too. For a gentrified mutt, he really was a supercilious little shit.

Paulie tilted the last of his beer down his throat and closed his eyes, letting the hot California sun bake his exertions into memory. The day was winding down. Soon the sun would duck behind the roof of the mansion and the pool would be left in shadow. Paulie was determined to enjoy the sunshine while he could get it.

As the heat of the sun and the gentle lapping of the water soothed away the pressures of the day, Paulie's mind was suddenly filled with thoughts of Ben. Ben naked. Lean and strong. Ben naked and trembling and thrusting his hard cock into Paulie's mouth. Ben gasping. Clutching.

Ben coming. Forever coming. The taste of his juices. The heat.

Eyes closed against the sun, Paulie felt his stiffening dick tent the soaked fabric of his swimming trunks. He was just about to reach down and give his cock a tweak when he heard a deep baritone voice not three feet away say, "Ahem."

Paulie swiftly flipped over onto his stomach, damn near snapping his dick off like an icicle in the process. He shielded his eyes against the glare and spotted Jeffrey standing at the edge of the pool looking down at him. There was a very sexy smile lighting Jeffrey's dark, handsome face.

Paulie could feel some of the blood which had migrated south to his pecker suddenly jump ship and head back up to his cheeks. In other words, he blushed.

"Oh, hi, Jeffrey. Uhhh, getting settled?"

"Yes sir. All ready to start my duties." He cast his eyes over Paulie's near-naked frame floating there at his feet. He looked like he might be a little disappointed Paulie had flipped over like he did. Apparently (in a biologist's parlance), the view of Paulie's anterior spectrum was a bit more interesting than the posterior spectrum. Although maybe not much. "For instance, sir, if there is anything I can help you with right now, I'd be more than happy to be of assistance."

The happy leer on the man's face made it pretty clear what he was talking about. And to say Paulie wasn't interested would have been a bold-faced lie.

But still, theirs had to be a working relationship or this whole houseboy thing wasn't going to work at all. Even Paulie had that much common sense, hard-on or no hard-on. And boy, didn't he hate himself for thinking *that* thought. Especially when he saw a rather impressive bulge in the crotch of Jeffrey's work uniform. The uniform looked rather like a nurse's scrubs, only snow white. Against Jeffrey's coffee skin, it was really quite fetching.

And so was the bulge. But still.

"No, uh—thanks, Jeffrey. Let me just get my robe, and I'll show you what you need to know." Although by the gleam in the man's eyes, Paulie suspected Jeffrey *already* knew everything he needed to know. Heh heh.

Jeffrey seemed slightly disappointed by what Paulie said, but he let it pass. Instead, he centered his attention on Hammer.

"The dog has his own raft." Jeffrey said it like a man who has just spotted an emu in the middle of church, passing around the collection plate.

Paulie looked over at Hammer, who was still obliviously gnawing on his giraffe and dangling his ass in the water off the back of the raft. His tail floated out behind him like a rudder. While he stared, Hammer gave a gaping yawn.

"Why?" Paulie asked, gazing back up at his handsome new houseboy. "You think it's too much?"

Chapter 3

PAULIE LEFT the mansion at ten o'clock the next morning to pick up the first arrivals at the airport. Jamie and Trevor and their two lovers, whom Paulie had yet to meet, were due to fly in at twelve. Paulie was leaving early because parking at Lindbergh Field was a bitch.

On his way out the door, Paulie said, "Toodles," to his scrumptious and dutiful new houseboy, who was towering over the kitchen sink in his sparkly white uniform and energetically washing the breakfast dishes. Apparently, he didn't believe in dishwashers.

But Jesus God, the man was handsome.

Paulie didn't know it, but Jeffrey was also trying to psyche himself up to running a final dustcloth over twenty-two rooms full of furniture and doodads. Jeffrey supposed that in rich circles, that was what it took to house one measly human—twenty-two rooms. Jeffrey had a look on his face that said white people sure do like to spread the fuck out. Where he came from you'd be more apt to see twenty-two humans in one room, rather than the other way around. And boy, did rich white people like to accumulate shit. Lordy, there was stuff everywhere. He'd be dusting until he was thirty.

Jeffrey might also have been a wee bit irked still that his advances, let us say in a *sexual* vein, had been politely but firmly spurned by his new boss. But hey, he told himself, he still had two weeks to work on getting the man in his clutches for a little one-on-one. And once he did, he fully intended to root around and take a peek at whatever was poking up under that sexy little bathing suit the man had been wearing the day before. The hungry look his new boss had cast at Jeffrey's expanding crotch hadn't been missed by Jeffrey either. Oh yeah. There was definitely hope yet for seducing the boss.

Thinking of Paulie sprawled out on that raft with a boner poking up like a flagpole made Jeffrey shift around on his feet to make room for Jeffrey Junior, who was in the process of meandering down his pant leg like a snake. A *big* snake. Jesus, his new boss was a looker.

When Paulie said, "Toodles," at the kitchen door, Jeffrey merely glanced back over his shoulder and gave the man a sudsy finger waggle back. No sense waving his hard-on around on his first day at work. Wouldn't want Paulie to think he was a perv or anything.

Hammer had been following Jeffrey around all morning like he was his new best friend. That was because Jeffrey had dropped a sausage as he was preparing Paulie's breakfast, which he was doing to test his own cooking skills, not because Paulie had asked him to. His cooking skills turned out to be just fine, as a matter of fact, although his serving skills needed a little work. Hammer had swooped in like a SCUD missile to gobble up that sausage before it ever hit the floor. Hammer had apparently mistaken the act of *dropping* for an act of *kindness*, and he had been praying for another act of kindness ever since. Now every time Jeffrey took a step to do *anything*, he was tripping over the dog.

Outside it was another glorious California day.

At the airport Paulie stood at the windows with a gazillion other people and watched Flight 223 from San Francisco bounce to a landing right on time. A few minutes later, he spotted Jamie and Trevor, arm in arm, bustling through the terminal, giggling and laughing and looking like they were having the time of their lives.

The two young men trailing along behind them looked a little less enthusiastic. They were pretty much ignoring each other and glowering around with sour expressions on their faces like their plane had just been hijacked to Ethiopia and Ethiopia was about the *last* place they wanted to be.

Those two were obviously the new lovers. And it was equally obvious they were not exactly thrilled that their recently acquired partners had discovered so much fun to be had in the company of their exes.

Apparently, Jamie and Trevor had been catching up on old times as they wended their way down the California coast at 35,000 feet, guzzling cocktails, noshing on peanuts, and probably playing footsies and kneesies along the way. Not to mention ignoring their boyfriends completely.

Paulie had to bite back a grin at the furious expressions worn by those two bringing up the rear. Jamie and Trevor were back in the saddle, stirring up shit already, just as they had in college. Paulie wondered if their relationships with their new partners would survive the gallop. Because even Paulie could see, at a distance of fifty feet and peering through the heads of those gazillion strangers, that Jamie and Trevor were already flirting with each other.

Well, good, Paulie thought. Maybe they'd get back together. Nothing would make Paulie happier. Those two belonged together, because frankly, nobody else could put up with them.

Paulie laughed out loud when the two looked up and spotted him in the crowd. They threw their arms in the air and took off running, screaming like maniacs and startling everyone in the terminal.

Two seconds later, Paulie was scooped up and spun around and the air squeezed out of him in a four-arm bear hug that came real close to popping a couple of ribs. By the time his friends were finished manhandling him, Paulie looked like he had been dragged behind a bus for a couple of blocks. His shirt was out, his hair was all over the place, and one of his shoes was missing. He was laughing so hard he had snot running out of his nose, and wasn't *that* a revolting development.

Jamie and Trevor finally held him out at arm's length to get a good look at him, and Trevor said, "Damn, Paulie. You look like crap!"

Jamie came to the rescue. "That's because we just mauled him." He reached into a pocket and pulled out a tissue, clamping it over Paulie's nose. "Blow," he said, like every doting mother who had ever walked the face of the earth.

So Paulie blew.

While he was doing that, some woman in the crowd handed him back his shoe.

During all this, the two trailing lovers were standing off to the side, arms folded across their chests, trying to appear like sports but actually just looking annoyed. After a while, even Jamie and Trevor seemed to finally feel the angry stares ricocheting off the backs of their heads like darts from a blowgun bouncing off a tree trunk.

Trevor and Jamie turned and dutifully motioned their lovers forward like a couple of teenage boys reluctantly presenting their ugly prom dates to their slightly startled (and disappointed) parents.

Apparently, Trevor was still in the mood for twisting knickers. He vaguely motioned to the two approaching young men and said to Paulie, "The one on the left is what's-his-name, and the one on the right is whoozit. Say hello to Paulie, guys."

Jamie slapped Trevor's arm. "Oh, don't be such a bitch. Paulie, this is my lover, um, wait, it'll come to me in a minute. And that's Trevor's lover. I have no idea what *his* fucking name is."

The two young men were getting redder by the second. Paulie decided détente was in order.

Still poking his shirt back into his pants, he stepped forward and clutched each of their hands in turn. "Ignore those clowns. I'm Paulie. It's great to have you here."

The two men shuffled their feet and tried to look a little friendlier. But it was all for Paulie's sake. It certainly wasn't meant for Jamie or Trevor.

Paulie gave them a sympathetic moue and hooked his thumb toward Trevor and Jamie, standing behind him. They were once again laughing and flirting and practically snogging each other as they ignored everyone else completely. "Those two been like this through the whole flight?"

"Yes," both men snapped in unison, and Paulie figured that was pretty much the end of *that* conversation.

Jamie and Trevor again turned their backs on their lovers, draping their arms over Paulie as they plowed their way through the crowd to the luggage carousel to pick up their bags.

"Very cute," Paulie whispered, so as not to be overheard by the two trailing sourpusses.

"Thanks," Jamie said. "I've been working out."

"No, I mean your boyfriends, dipshit. I still don't know who belongs to who, of course. Don't suppose it matters at this point. They're so pissed off your relationships are probably doomed anyway."

Trevor shrugged. "Yeah, well, sometimes people should just lighten up."

Paulie glanced back. The two abandoned lovers seemed to have finally decided having one ally on their side of the war was better than none, so they were speaking to each other, although they didn't look exactly thrilled about it.

Both men were handsome, although one of them was a little effeminate for Paulie's taste, with his salon-frosted hair and perfect spray tan and Abercrombie & Fitch traveling ensemble. That one probably belonged to Jamie. Jamie had always had a preference for readily fuckable men. The other, the more butch of the two, looked more like Trevor's type. He was truly a knockout, but appeared awfully young. If he was even twenty-one, Paulie would be surprised. And now he thought about it, even the younger man looked pretty readily fuckable.

In Paulie's opinion, his two friends looked far more at home and far happier in the company of each other than they would ever be in the company of the two snotheads sulking in the rear. Trevor and Jamie's breakup had been diva-esque and loud and heart crushing for both of them, Paulie knew. But now they were back together again, at least for the next couple of weeks, Paulie had a feeling they might start rethinking the decision they had made to split up three months out of college.

Paulie suspected there would be a couple of broken hearts to contend with before these next two weeks ground to a halt. And he seriously doubted those broken hearts would belong to his friends.

Then out of nowhere, Ben's face flashed across his mind, and Paulie wondered if maybe his own heart would be the third to bite the dust.

At least his two goofy friends, Jamie and Trevor, hadn't been fools enough to fall for a straight guy.

They both had enough sense to avoid being *that* stupid.

BY THE time they were in the parking lot loading the car with enough luggage to fill a tour bus, Paulie had learned the names of the two lovers. They were Danny and Jack. Danny was the one who looked like he should still be in high school. Jack was Abercrombie & Fitch. The surliness on Danny's and Jack's faces intensified yet again when Trevor and Jamie piled happily into the front seat with Paulie, leaving the other two to huddle neglected in the back like a couple of side orders of asparagus nobody really wanted. Paulie figured their dour expressions would at least save him a little gas. They were putting out such a cold air of discord, Paulie wouldn't need to run the air conditioner on the way home.

In the car, Trevor and Jamie cranked down the silliness long enough to tell Paulie how sorry they had been to hear about his grandmother's death.

"She was a great lady," Trevor said.

"And a hoot," Jamie added with a fond smile. "She sure loved the hell out of us."

Paulie laughed. "She sure did. But then, who doesn't?"

Somebody in the back seat coughed around the word "Horseshit."

Everybody in the front seat ignored it.

"So…," Trevor cooed, reaching over Jamie's back and running seductive fingers through Paulie's tangled hair, damn near yanking Paulie's head off in the process. "Left everything to *you*, did she? La Jolla mansion, humongous bank account, stocks and bonds, fur coats, Hammer."

"Hammer was already mine, and the fur coats are too small."

"What a shame," Trevor tutted.

Jack leaned over the front seat, annoying everyone, breathing down their necks, and trying to see himself in the rearview mirror. Maybe he was afraid his mascara was clumping. Once he was reasonably satisfied he was still lovely, he plopped back down by the rear door and stared out the side window, looking bored. He was obviously being snippy when he asked, "So your grandmother left you a hammer?"

Paulie chuckled at that while Trevor and Jamie rolled their eyes, which wasn't lost on Jack either. Paulie felt the temperature drop a couple more degrees.

"No," Paulie explained. "Hammer's my dog."

"Last time I visited," Jamie said, "Hammer humped my leg until he squirted jism on my ankle."

"I remember doing that to you a few times," Trevor interjected. "You didn't seem to mind."

"Yeah, but this was *dog* jism. Eww. I felt so cheap."

"You are cheap," Trevor said, and they both howled with laughter.

Paulie snuck a peek in the mirror at the faces in the back. Nary a smile.

Tough room, he thought. *This is going to be fun.*

As Paulie pulled onto the circular drive in front of the mansion, a rather interesting silence suddenly descended on the occupants of the car. It was like Maxwell Smart had dropped the Cone of Silence over the proceedings. Looking around, Paulie realized all four of his guests were staring through the front windshield like a pack of hungry dogs eyeing a meatloaf.

Gazing ahead to see what was so interesting, Paulie spotted Jeffrey, standing at the portico by the front door, hands clasped behind his back, regal black head held aloft, chin high, watching the Ford approach like it was a hansom cab carting the Queen Mother in for tea, and he was there to help her safely alight.

Paulie tried not to laugh. The guy was playing his part to the hilt, and his performance wasn't lost on anybody. Neither was his physique. Tall, brooding demeanor. Handsome-as-hell face. Broad shoulders. Slim hips. Long, long legs. And something lying all bunched up under the fly of his snow-white trousers that looked like it was trying to bust out and make a run for it.

"My God," Danny said, hanging over the front seat and practically drooling. "Look at the basket on the butler."

"He's not the butler." Paulie grinned. "He's the houseboy."

"Houseboy, my ass," Jamie sighed. "Househunk is more like it."

"A Nubian slave," Jack said with a trembly breath as he once again checked his mascara in the rearview mirror. "I'm gonna get *me* one of those."

Paulie really laughed at that. "Call him a Nubian slave and you'll be fishing your head out of the pool. Best to just call him Jeffrey. You'll live longer."

"Gotcha," Jack cooed. "The forceful type. Love that."

"You certainly do," Jamie droned, rolling his eyes so far up into his head they practically slid down the back of his shirt.

"Oh hush," Jack said, slapping Jamie's shoulder in the first show of good humor Paulie had seen from the guy. Although Paulie had to admit seeing Jeffrey looking so gorgeous standing there on his front porch with his bigass basket and smiling face cheered him up too.

Trevor laid his head on Paulie's shoulder and gazed up at him with doe eyes while he snuggled close. "I want to live like you do, Paulie. Mansion, money, houseboy. Marry me."

Danny snarled from the back seat. "You're already married, asshole."

Paulie shot a questioning look in Trevor's direction as if to ask, "Married?"

Trevor scrunched up his face and gave his head a determined shake, mouthing the word, "No."

Jamie dragged his eyes away from the houseboy's crotch long enough to take in everything else. "Still living in a hovel, I see. You'd think you'd have traded up by now. Maybe got a condo in the suburbs."

"You must be kidding!" Jack gushed, also tearing his eyes away from Jeffrey long enough to scope out the property. "This place is *fabulous!*"

"As a matter of fact," Jamie mumbled. "I *was* kidding." And in an even softer mumble, he added, "Twit."

As soon as Paulie pulled up to the front steps, Jeffrey opened the driver's door and offered Paulie a helping hand out of the vehicle. He let everyone else fend for himself.

Paulie gave him a subdued snarl, just to let him know he was being a little too unctuous, but Jeffrey just beamed innocently back at him and slid a seductive thumb over the tender skin of Paulie's palm as he pulled him from the car.

Danny jumped from the back seat and sucked in a deep breath of air. "Damn, I can smell the ocean! We must be close."

"Just out the back door." Paulie smiled, yanking his hand out of Jeffrey's and trying to be a gracious host. Danny was looking so eager and young and handsome that Paulie was beginning to see what must have attracted Trevor to him in the first place.

Danny gave a good-natured groan. "Oh man, I should have brought my surfboard."

"Yeah," Trevor groused, "like we didn't bring *enough* luggage."

"Don't worry," Paulie said, laughing. "You can borrow mine." He glared at Jeffrey, who was now gently smoothing the wrinkles out of Paulie's shirt and brushing imaginary lint off Paulie's shoulders like a good little house elf should.

Paulie cleared his throat. "Whenever you're through schmoozing the boss, Studly, how about a hand with the bags?"

"Yes, massa." Jeffrey grinned, eyeballing Paulie like a fox salivating over a nice plump chicken. Then, with a sigh, he toddled his six foot six inches off to the back of the car.

Jack seemed to have permanently recovered his good humor, and all it had taken was a gander at the houseboy's crotch. He did a nelly little wrist flap and gushed, "I'll just help Jeffrey with the bags. He shouldn't have to do it all by his little lonesome."

The next thing Paulie knew, Jeffrey and Jack had their heads in the trunk, and Jack was flirting and giggling and oohing and aahing over the size of Jeffrey's biceps. If it bothered Jamie, he sure didn't show it. He grabbed Trevor with one arm, Paulie with the other, and steered them toward the house.

"It's cocktail hour," he said. "I didn't fly all this way to watch my boyfriend hit on the househunk."

"He is a bit effeminate, isn't he?" Trevor dryly commented. "Your boyfriend, I mean."

Jamie grinned. "He has his uses." Then he cast his eyes at Danny, who was standing at the side of the car as if he didn't quite know what he should do. "That one looks like he has his uses too. How are his grades? Is he doing his homework on time? Must be an exciting time for him moving up to high school and all."

Trevor giggled. "Oh, shut up." Lowering his voice to a whisper, he added, "The boy has a lovely ass. Not much going on upstairs, but intelligence is highly overrated anyway. That's why you and I always got along so well."

"Blow me," Jamie said.

And Trevor simpered, "Now? Don't you think we should unpack first?"

Paulie ushered them through the front door. Danny had wandered toward the side yard, perhaps trying to catch a glimpse of the ocean.

As they climbed the stairs to the second floor, still arm in arm in arm, Trevor asked, "When's Ben getting in? We're a Musketeer short."

Paulie felt his heart do a little jig inside his chest. Jesus, even hearing the guy's name did a number on him. "He said he'd be here when he gets here. He's driving in."

"From Omaha? You're kidding."

Paulie shrugged. "That's what he said in his letter."

Paulie had been wondering why Ben had chosen to drive as well. A horrible thought suddenly plowed through his head like a runaway train smashing through a depot. Christ, he hoped Ben hadn't gone and fallen for some broad and now was dead set on taking her on a cross-country road trip with the final intention of showing her off to his gay friends in California.

Paulie stopped dead in his tracks when that thought hit him. And when he stopped, he dragged Trevor and Jamie to a stop too.

"What?" They both asked. "You okay?"

Paulie just shook it off. "Somebody must have walked over my grave. It's nothing."

"Weirdo," Trevor said as Paulie shepherded him into the first bedroom.

"This is yours, Trevor. Yours and Danny's. Jamie, you and Abercrom—I mean, Jack, will be in the room across the hall. I'm going to go help with your bags and make sure my househunk isn't making passes at the guests." *Not that the guests looked like they would much mind if he did.*

The minute he stepped out of Trevor and Jamie's grasp, the two walked smack into each other's arms. They didn't even wait for Paulie to leave the room.

"I've missed you babe," Trevor said.

"Same here," Jamie answered.

And just before they kissed, Paulie had the good sense to close the door as he stepped from the room, just in case Jamie's and Trevor's lovers should walk by.

Yep, he thought, *it's going to be a hell of a two weeks.*

When the thought of Ben dragging a woman across country with him hit Paulie again, he had an almost uncontrollable urge to plop his ass down on the top step and cry like a baby.

Paulie hated the bitch already, and he didn't even know if she existed.

How fucking nutso was that?

Of course, Ben wouldn't bring along an extra guest without telling him, would he? Ben had more manners than that. Unless he wanted to surprise everybody. Then he might. Damn!

Paulie heard a squeal of laughter and leaned over the bannister to gaze down at the foyer. Coming up the stairs was Jeffrey with a humongous suitcase in one hand, another suitcase under his arm, and Jack tossed over his shoulder like a sack of potatoes. Jeffrey's free arm had burrowed between Jack's legs and his hand was centered squarely over Jack's ass. Jack had his nose down the back of Jeffrey's shirt like a hog rooting for truffles.

Jeffrey also seemed to be limping. Looking closer, Paulie saw his houseboy had a hard-on poking down his pant leg. If he wasn't careful, he would trip on it coming up the stairs. Golly, it reached halfway to his knee.

Jeffrey looked up and spotted Paulie. He stretched his mouth out in a smile that brought every one of those gorgeous teeth into play. Paulie was almost blinded by the glare.

Jeffrey's laughter boomed up the stairs. "I told him I could bench press two hundred pounds, but he wouldn't believe me."

Jack pulled his face out of Jeffrey's collar and looked up with a sexy little smirk on his face. "Now I do!"

Jeffrey gave his ass a friendly pat. A friendly *lingering* pat.

"Where's Danny?" Paulie asked, trying to get Jeffrey's attention, desperately tilting his head to the side to keep him from dragging Jack up the stairs to where Jamie and Trevor were doing God-knows-what in the bedroom.

"He's skinny-dipping in the pool," Jack squealed. Jeffrey had just poked a long finger into the back of Jack's pants, obviously reconnoitering the terrain. Jack seemed to like being reconnoitered. He was doing a little ass dance under Jeffrey's big broad hand, squirming around, oohing and aahing, and maybe even humping Jeffrey's shoulder a little bit like Hammer probably would if he could get his dick up that high. Paulie couldn't really blame Jack either. If Jeffrey had his hand all over Paulie's ass, Paulie would probably be happily squirming around too. Only he liked to think he wouldn't be so nelly about it.

Paulie stopped fantasizing and grabbed a plan out of midair. In love and war, when you see an opening, you just have to take it. "Jeffrey, Jack, you boys go skinny-dipping too, if you want. Just leave the bags on the stairs. Go on now. We can bring them up later. Go enjoy the pool."

Jeffrey dropped the bags before Paulie finished talking. With Jack still on his shoulder, Jeffrey kicked off his shoes and tried to reach down to peel off his socks. He took off down the stairs and toward the kitchen with his simpering cargo still draped across his shoulder. Jeffrey shrugged out of his shirt as he went.

Paulie wasn't sure if he had just prevented a disaster or caused one.

He raced back down the hallway to the bedroom and quietly pushed open the door.

Christ! Trevor and Jamie were stone cold naked. Jamie was on his knees with Trevor's cock in his mouth, and Trevor was hanging onto

Jamie's head like it was a bowling ball and one more strike would win him the tournament.

Paulie closed the door before they noticed he was there. Actually, a brass band could probably have marched through with a couple of elephants and a shitload of clowns, and they wouldn't have known *they* were there either.

With everyone around him naked, or nearly naked, or downright having sex, Paulie began to feel a little left out.

He headed for the bar and poured himself two fingers of scotch. Neat. He downed it in two seconds flat and poured himself another.

As the booze burned a path through his guts to his spleen and all points beyond, he found himself wondering when Ben would get in.

And what exactly would happen when he did? Would there be an awkward few minutes when Ben remembered all that had happened the last time he was with Paulie? Or instead of lasting just a few minutes, would the awkwardness never end? Would Paulie find himself apologizing over and over for that horrible breach of etiquette when Paulie stuck his face in Ben's crotch and began chewing on the most beautiful cock in the world? After all, he had been apologizing for it inside his head for the past two years. Maybe it was time he actually apologized to Ben in person. Or would Ben have a woman with him and be so in love with her he didn't even *remember* what Paulie had done two years earlier in a moment of drunken lust.

Drunken lust on *both* their parts. For even now, Paulie remembered Ben clutching his hips and pressing his lips to the base of Paulie's cock while Ben trembled and shook and his ass came off the bed as his come splattered Paulie's face, Paulie's throat, Paulie's hair. Paulie could still feel it. God, Paulie could still *taste* it. The sweetest come he had ever tasted in his life.

And what he wouldn't give to taste it again.

Paulie downed the second two fingers of scotch and headed for the car. He'd bring in the luggage himself.

Maybe it would take his mind off Ben.

Yeah, right. Like that would work. Then he looked down.

Well, phooey. Now, like all his houseguests and the help, he had a hard-on too. It seemed to be going around. Sort of an epidemic.

Please God, let it go away. I can't think with this hard-on thumping in my crotch. And while you're at it, God, please don't let Ben drag a woman into the middle of all this. My poor wounded heart couldn't take it. I'd have to kill the bitch. And you know you wouldn't like that. I'm trying to take your feelings into account, God. Play along with me here. Okay? Please?

Crap.

Chapter 4

PAULIE WAS getting woozy. He wasn't sure if it was from the scotch
or the sun or from watching his newly acquired houseboy frolic naked
in the pool with the equally naked Danny and Jack.

Jack was a delight to look at: spray-tanned to the hilt, of course,
but still very nicely put together for a raging queen. Smooth, lean body,
hairless legs, tight little butt. He had the habit of holding his nose and
squeezing his eyes shut when he ducked his head under the water.
Paulie tried not to laugh every time he watched him do it. Johnny
Weissmuller the guy wasn't.

Danny was damned enticing too, with his slim, youthful surfer's
body. Unlike Jack's, Danny's skin was radiantly and healthily
weathered. Clearly the man was bronzed from the sun. He hadn't been
chemically treated in a tanning booth at forty bucks a pop. His body
was smooth from the waist up and fuzzy from the waist down. And also
unlike Jack, Danny moved through the water effortlessly, as graceful
and lithe as a guppy. Paulie suspected Danny loved swimming just as
much as Paulie loved running. He was breathtaking to watch, moving
smoothly over the water or beneath it, breaching like a dolphin, then
floating on his back with his young dick poking straight up into the air
like a ship's mast just begging for somebody to hang a flag on it.

But my God, Jeffrey was the most stunning man Paulie had ever
seen, aside from Ben. Jeffrey was hung like a horse, his six-foot-six
physique was flawless, and his gentle creamed-coffee coloring made
you want to slide a finger down his ribcage, then pop it in your mouth

just to see what the man tasted like. Caramel, maybe? Nougat? Creamy chocolate fudge?

Of course, no one could compete with Ben when it came to pure beauty. But Paulie had to admit, Jeffrey ran a close second.

Trevor and Jamie didn't seem averse to watching Jeffrey cavorting naked either. And they also didn't seem to much mind that Paulie's houseboy and their two boyfriends were having everything but a three-way fuck fest in the pool. For one thing, aside from Paulie and Trevor and Jamie, there wasn't a swimsuit in sight. And for another thing, with Paulie and Trevor and Jamie *included,* there wasn't a man on the property who wasn't sporting a boner.

Paulie was trying to ignore his own hard-on, while Jamie had rested a proprietary hand over Trevor's as the two lay side by side at the edge of the pool on lounge chairs, sipping mimosas. Paulie had stuck to scotch. Jamie's fingers were gently patting and tweaking the head of Trevor's dick through the fabric of Trevor's swimming trunks in an absentminded sort of way while they talked. Paulie could see Trevor making a concerted effort to follow the conversation and at the same time not grind his crotch into his ex's hot little hand, but it looked like an uphill battle—a battle Paulie was pretty sure Trevor was going to lose sooner or later.

My God, Paulie thought, they just had sex upstairs not twenty minutes ago. Didn't they ever get enough? Or maybe Paulie was just jealous. He hadn't had sex with a human other than himself for—what, weeks? Now there was a depressing thought. He swallowed a little more scotch in an attempt to drown it.

Both Trevor and Jamie had kept themselves in shape. Trevor was toned from long hours at the gym, as he always had been in college, and Jamie, like Paulie, was a runner. Both men had strong hairy legs and broad chests, Trevor's pelted with hair, Jamie's smooth but with a very enticing trail of fuzz leading down across his stomach and disappearing beneath the waistband of his trunks. Needless to say, Paulie enjoyed looking at both of them. They were very sexy guys.

Paulie was drinking fast because he loved motioning for Jeffrey to drag his luscious body and stiff dick out of the pool every ten minutes to hustle off to the cabana to pour him another scotch. And to Jeffrey's credit, he didn't seem to mind doing it. Paulie suspected it was only because he was having fun waving his big dick in Paulie's face every time he leaned over to serve him another drink.

Paulie was enjoying it too; don't think he wasn't. He was already wondering how he could sneak down the hall in the middle of the night to the houseboy's room without his guests finding out. Not that they would care, he supposed. But still—it didn't seem the Amy Vanderbilt thing to do. He could almost hear her now: "A hostess simply does not fuck the help. It isn't done. And if it is done, then it must be done very very quietly. Yet with great gusto."

Just when Paulie was beginning to reacquire a sense of propriety as far as his hostessing duties were concerned, along came Jeffrey with another scotch for him and a couple of mimosas for Jamie and Trevor, waving that gigantic uncut erection all over the place.

Christ, Paulie wasn't made of steel after all. His dick sorta was at the moment, but *he* wasn't.

During all this, Hammer lay in the shade under Paulie's lounge chair, sprawled out on a towel, snoring like a lumberjack. When he snored, he sounded like a giant snorkle.

Jamie tapped Paulie on the arm as soon as Jeffrey's houseboy duties were fulfilled and everyone was slurping on nice fresh drinks. Before speaking, Jamie watched Jeffrey cannonball back into the pool, flashing that perfect ass of his and causing both Jack and Danny to squeal in mock terror.

When the show was over, Jamie turned away from the pool and said, "So tell us what happened between you and Ben. You've kept the secret long enough. Spill."

Paulie tried on an innocent face, wondering how it looked. It seemed to fit okay, so he left it in place. "What makes you think anything happened between me and Ben?"

Trevor snorted a laugh. "The man disappeared, that's why. He disappeared during the commencement exercises, and he hasn't been seen since. We haven't heard from him, and unless I'm mistaken, you haven't heard from him either. You must have done something to piss him off."

Paulie could feel the blood rushing to his face. Unless he was in the throes of an orgasm, he wasn't fond of that feeling. "But I did hear from him. He contacted me after my grandmother's death. That's when

I invited him here with us for these next two weeks, and that's when he said yes, and that's why we're all lying around with hard-ons waiting for him. I assume he's been busy between then and now, teaching in Omaha, carving out a life for himself. It's what he always wanted, to be a teacher. I'm sure he's having the time of his life."

Just saying those words was a little like sticking a hatpin into his own heart. How could Ben be having the time of his life without Paulie? How *could* he? The prick. And Omaha? Who the fuck moves to Omaha?

Paulie pushed those thoughts away as quickly as they came. Good grief, Ben had been out of his life for almost two years. How could Paulie still be having these thoughts? And Ben was straight, for Christ's sake. *Straight.*

Before either of his friends could wheedle any further information out of him, Paulie decided to wheedle some of his own, just to change the subject.

"So tell me, Trevor, is Danny your new love?" He tried not to look at Trevor's bulging crotch with Jamie's hand still resting on it while he spoke.

Trevor shielded his eyes from the sun and looked out across the water at Danny, who at the moment was sitting atop Jeffrey's broad shoulders with his fuzzy tanned legs clamped around Jeffrey's head. Jeffrey was holding those young legs with his strong hands. Holding them tight. While they watched, Danny twisted away, planted his feet firmly on either side of Jeffrey's shoulders, stood up, and executed a perfect backflip into the water. Paulie felt like holding up a little card with the number 10 printed on it, as much for the dive as for the kid's beauty. Plus, he had never seen anyone do a backflip with an erection before. It was really quite breathtaking.

Trevor was smiling fondly at the kid as he resurfaced, grinning and spouting water like a whale.

"Danny's a sweet kid. We get along great. He moved in with me a couple of months ago, and he seems content to call himself my lover. He's dynamite in bed."

"Does he work?" Paulie asked, wondering how Jamie felt about the things Trevor was saying. If he was jealous, he had the good sense not to let Trevor know.

"He's a waiter at a popular restaurant on the Wharf. Does pretty well at it. His service probably sucks, but he's cute enough to rake in the tips. We do live in San Francisco, you know. Fruitcup Central. People who look like Danny can always make a go of it there." He gazed back out at the water with a gentle smile on his face. "He's a good kid. Very sweet. And sexy as hell, obviously."

Paulie turned to Jamie. "And Jack? What's the story behind him?"

Jamie's smile had slipped away while Trevor spoke. He had also removed his hand from the bulge in Trevor's bathing suit. Trevor didn't look too happy about seeing it go.

"We have a perfect synergy, Jack and I. Jack loves to get fucked. I love to fuck. There you have it in a nutshell." His words were clipped, terse, and emotionless.

Paulie urged him on. "So you live together?"

"Not yet, but he wants to."

"Do you love him?" It was Trevor who asked the question. "Or is he just another flavor of the week? You know, like you used to treat yourself to on the sly when we were together."

Paulie watched as Jamie focused solely on Trevor's face, his eyes burning deep into Trevor's stare. Paulie could almost feel Jamie erasing all outside stimuli, the three romping in the pool, the sensation of his own stiff cock pressing against the fabric of his swim trunks, the sound of Jack squealing yet again in the pool as Jeffrey lifted him high and tossed his naked ass across the water.

"No," Jamie said to Trevor alone. "I don't love him. He's just— convenient."

In a hushed voice, Trevor asked, "Does he love you?"

And Jamie shrugged. "You'd have to ask him that question."

Trevor's eyes were lasers now. His face was getting red, and Paulie didn't think it was from the sun.

"So does *Jack* work?"

"He's a hairdresser."

"Gee." Trevor chuckled, looking out at the pool again, where Jack was cuddling up to Jeffrey's naked back and hanging onto the man like a coat on a coat hanger. "A hairdresser. Now there's a surprise."

Jamie laughed a mean-spirited little laugh. "It beats busing tables."

"Waiting. *Waiting* tables."

"Whatever."

Trevor threw Jamie's snark right back in his face. "Yeah. Whatever."

Suddenly all humor seemed to have left the conversation. "Blow me," Jamie snarled.

Trevor gave him an innocent look. "What? *Again?*"

Paulie didn't like the way things were progressing here. He thought it might be prudent to get the hell away from these two before the fireworks really started. After all, it's always the innocent bystander who ends up with a bullet in his head.

He glanced at his watch. Almost four. When the hell was Ben going to arrive? And if he did arrive, how was anyone going to hear him ring the bell on the front gate a mile and a half away? Fucking mansion.

Paulie decided to take his dick and go. He'd had enough temptation for one day. Besides, he had a hunch Jamie and Trevor were about to do a little soul-searching between themselves. Or fist fighting. One or the other. The last thing Paulie wanted to do was witness either one.

He politely excused himself, grabbed a towel to cover the embarrassing tent pole in his trunks, and hustled off to the house.

He jumped in the shower to wash off the pool chemicals and precome—after all, his dick had been dripping fluid for the last hour while Paulie ogled all the naked men cavorting in the pool. After his shower, he took a few minutes to style his hair properly with a blow dryer and brush. It would be nice to sober up and look halfway decent when Ben arrived.

Paulie suddenly realized how nervous he was. Jeez, he was like a schoolgirl on her first date. And it wasn't even a date. It was a reunion. A simple reunion of college buddies. Old friends. That's all it was.

Then once again, Paulie froze in place in front of the bathroom mirror, remembering Ben on that last night they had been together. How he felt, how he looked, how he tasted. Ben's total acceptance of Paulie's lips and hands on his body. On his cock.

It was still an amazing thing to Paulie: Ben's acceptance of him that night. Letting Paulie do what he did. Cross the line. Make a pass. Go all the way. Of course, Ben was snockered. They'd been drinking for hours. That was the short explanation right there. And the fact that Ben had taken a powder in either shame or anger the minute he sobered up pretty well put the lie to any hope on Paulie's part that Ben had actually enjoyed what had taken place.

Frankly, Paulie still couldn't understand why Ben had accepted Paulie's invitation to visit. Had Paulie been forgiven? Had Ben decided to let bygones be bygones? Had Ben's shame dissipated to a point where he thought he could now face his friends again?

Paulie didn't know the answer to any of those questions, but he supposed he'd be learning the truth sooner or later. He'd just have to wait for Ben to fill him in.

Paulie closed his eyes, took a deep breath to clear his head of booze and doubt and memories, and headed off to his bedroom to dress, donning shorts and a T-shirt for the evening. Fuck it. These were his friends. He wasn't entertaining POTUS and FLOTUS.

The caterers would be arriving soon with dinner. The least he could do would be greet them at the kitchen door sober, like a respectable client instead of a drunken, horny, homosexual, lovesick sot.

Jeez. Try saying *that* ten times really fast after downing half a bottle of scotch.

PAULIE WAS happy to learn he had chosen his caterers just as wisely as the agency had chosen his houseboy. Dinner was great. Nice and simple, just as Paulie preferred. Prime rib, au gratin potatoes, baby peas, a heavenly Caesar salad, and ice cream cake to top it all off. Paulie decided to ask the caterers to cut back on the calories next time, but for their first dinner together, the choice was excellent. And they were all starving.

Jeffrey informed Paulie he would be more than happy to serve the meal, so Paulie sent the catering party off as soon as the food was delivered. After seeing how drunk everyone was, they didn't seem too averse to the idea of leaving. Paulie couldn't say he blamed them.

Especially since Jack and Danny were still roaming around the mansion as naked as jaybirds.

Jeffrey had at least donned trousers to serve dinner, but he was still shirtless and barefoot. Paulie didn't mind. He enjoyed the view. No one standing on ceremony here. No sir.

Jack seemed to be enjoying the view of the half-naked houseboy too. He was simpering all over Jeffrey and ignoring Jamie completely. No doubt he was still upset with the way Jamie and Trevor had spent the afternoon fawning all over each other. Although Paulie had to admit, it looked like the fawning was finally over. Jamie was centering all his attention on Paulie now, ignoring Trevor completely, and Trevor was looking a little hurt and confused about it. Paulie suspected the kind words Trevor had spoken earlier about Danny were to blame. Jamie was jealous, pure and simple, and Trevor was too dense to realize it.

Paulie decided he'd fill him in the first chance he got. Maybe Trevor could reverse the damage he'd done if he would simply stop praising his new boyfriend in front of his old one. Never politic that. Never a good idea.

Aside from the two naked boyfriends and the half-clad houseboy, everyone else had donned respectable shorts and tees for dinner, although Paulie suspected if the booze kept flowing the way it had been, even those few shreds of clothing would be flying out the window pretty soon.

Thank God his grandmother was dead. She'd have a conniption fit seeing Jack's and Danny's naked asses plopped down on her needlepointed dining room chairs. It wouldn't matter how cute the asses were. In his grandmother's eyes, had she still been alive, he suspected an ass would be simply… an ass. The esthetic beauty of said ass lost in the ravages of old age and forgotten libido.

Paulie couldn't help wondering how Ben would react to all this naked manflesh running around the mansion. Perhaps he should put a stop to it now before Ben's arrival. It would certainly make it more comfortable for Ben.

Paulie tapped his wineglass with a fork. Everybody immediately shushed and looked at him like they did in the movies when somebody pinged their wineglass for attention. *What do you know?* Paulie thought. *It works.*

Paulie stood and held out his glass in a toast. "I'm glad you're all here, guys. It's going to be an interesting two weeks, I can tell already. There is, however, going to be a slight change in the house rules."

Trevor looked at Jamie, Danny looked at Jack, Jeffrey looked at everyone in turn.

Not entirely joking, Paulie suspected, Jack piped up with, "So are we all going to sleep in the same bed, then?" He eyed Jeffrey while he said it. Apparently, he had forgotten about Jamie completely. And Paulie really couldn't blame him. Jamie certainly wasn't paying Jack any attention either.

Paulie spit up a good-natured laugh, although secretly he thought Jack was the biggest slut he'd ever seen. Nice ass, though.

"Nothing like that." Paulie smiled, taking a moment to sip his wine. "But we have another guest coming, and I'd like to assure him a comfortable visit. A straight guest. So for Ben's sake, let's all don at least *something* to wear when we're inside the mansion. The pool can stay optional. Skinny-dipping never hurt anybody, as long as we're not actually fucking on the diving board. So Danny, Jack, this is your last nude dinner. That okay?"

Danny gave Paulie an affable shrug, and Jack lifted his glass to toast his agreement. Jamie and Trevor said nothing, since they weren't the ones sitting around naked on Paulie's grandmother's dining room chairs anyway.

Paulie thought Jeffrey looked a bit disappointed, so he said, "Jeffrey, you are free to use the pool anytime you like in any state of dress or undress you desire when your duties offer you a chance, and I'm sure that will be often. I'm not exactly working you to death here. Deal?"

Jeffrey flashed his choppers. "Deal, sir."

Paulie nodded and turned back to his guests. "Thanks, everybody. I'm sure this one little rule won't ruin anyone's good time. So have fun and do anything else you want. The joint is yours."

Paulie plopped his ass back down in the chair, glad that was over.

Jamie reached out and patted his arm. "You did great. Very butch. Very forceful. You should be an orator. Public speaking is definitely your forte."

"Screw you," Paulie said around a grin.

"Maybe later," Jamie droned. "Right now I'm a little tired. I'm not sure why."

"Probably from cruising your ex all day," Jack mumbled into his cake, but still loud enough for everyone to hear.

And since no one could think of an argument to it, no one pretended to take offense.

AFTER ANOTHER couple of gallons of alcohol bit the dust, the evening finally wound itself down to an end.

Paulie was glad to see that as bedtime approached, the couples finally began to gravitate toward the people they came with. Jack with Jamie, Danny with Trevor. All out nuclear war between the battling factions seemed to have been somehow averted, at least for today. God knows what tomorrow would bring.

Still playing his role as houseboy with perfect aplomb, at least when he wasn't bareass naked and frolicking with the guests, Jeffrey cleared away the mess from dinner, then turned down everyone's beds and even placed a mint on their pillows, all the while humming and looking absolutely stunning while he did it. Paulie didn't know where the hell Jeffrey got the mints. Did he bring them with him? Was he that devoted to his work?

With the house finally still, and alone for the first time all day, Paulie breathed a sigh of relief as he peeled off his clothes and crawled wearily into bed. Sucking on his own mint, he switched off the bedside light and stared up at the dark ceiling, wondering what had happened to Ben. He supposed driving from Omaha to La Jolla wasn't something you could time to the minute, so it probably wouldn't be appropriate to start worrying yet. If Paulie knew Ben's cell phone number, he could call him and find out what was going on, but since he didn't, he would simply have to wait.

The oil tanker full of scotch he had consumed during the course of the day began to pull Paulie into sleep. Even his original idea of sneaking down the hall to jump the houseboy was forgotten. He was just too damned tired.

With the mint still melting on his tongue, and with soft voices wafting through the walls, either from Jamie's or Trevor's room, Paulie's breathing slowed. His eyes closed.

The next thing he knew, he was dreaming. Dreaming of Ben. Reliving that night so long ago.

Even in his dream, it was without a doubt the greatest and worst night of his life. Great because he finally scrounged up the courage to taste what he had always wanted to taste, and worst because he lost a friend doing it.

When a bell began jangling in his dream, Paulie blinked himself awake and sat straight up in bed. That's when he realized the jangling bell wasn't part of his dream at all.

It was the doorbell on the front gate.

Paulie knew beyond all doubt whose finger had pressed the bell. He gazed blearily through half-open eyes at the field of stars through the bedroom window. The moon hung high in the sky. It was late. Like early morning late. Three o'clock maybe. Or four. Then he had the good sense to check the clock on the nightstand. Yep. Three o'clock.

While Paulie considered that, Hammer started howling from somewhere at the base of the stairs, trying to get his attention. Like he wasn't awake already.

Heart banging away inside his chest as if he were suffering from stage fright, Paulie dragged on his shorts and shirt and took a gander at himself in the dresser mirror. Great. He looked and felt like he had just fallen out of a cyclone. Hair sticking straight up, eyes baggy and bloodshot from all the scotch he'd consumed, five o'clock shadow, possum breath. Oh well. Too late to worry about it now. He stumbled down the stairs as quietly as he could so as not to wake anyone else. He wanted to see Ben for the first time alone. For some reason that was very important. He needed just a quiet minute to look at the man. Just look at him.

Descending the stairs, he shushed Hammer, who took off running for the front door, tail wagging, tongue lolling. He thought he was going for a walk.

Paulie unlocked the front door and stepped out into the night. The walkway was cold beneath his bare feet, the night air cool on his legs. The dew on the garden sparkled in the moonlight, and he could smell the cypress trees in the backyard. Hammer took off running across the lawn toward the rear of the house. He had forgotten the bell already, forgotten why they were outside at all. Brainless mutt.

Paulie reached for the handle on the front gate and flicked the lock with his thumb. Sucking in a deep breath of air to calm his fluttering heart, he pulled open the gate.

Chapter 5

AND THERE stood Ben. Alone and handsome beneath the light in the archway.

For some reason, Ben was staring down at Paulie's bare feet.

"You lost a toenail," Ben said. Then he raised his eyes to Paulie's face. His lips were twisted into a gentle smile that made Paulie feel like a million bucks. Paulie had waited a long time to see that smile again. Ben tsked then and added, "Runners."

"Ever beat the five minute mile?" Paulie asked, still relishing the sight of that beautiful smile.

"Fuck no. You?"

"Fuck no."

They laughed.

Again Ben looked down at Paulie's poor toe. "I lost a toenail myself about two weeks ago. A big one. Just like you."

Paulie grinned. "If that's all you lost, then I guess we're okay."

It was out of Paulie's mouth before he could stop himself. Paulie hadn't meant it as a double entendre, but even in his own mind, it immediately dredged up the memory of their last night together. If it dredged up the same memory for Ben, and the damage that night had done to their relationship, or what Paulie *perceived* as damage, Ben wasn't letting on. He barked out a laugh and scooped Paulie into his arms. The hug was undoubtedly brotherly on Ben's side, but Paulie didn't quite see it that way. Suddenly finding himself in the arms he had been dreaming about for the past two years would have knocked his socks off had he been wearing any. Paulie closed his eyes and savored every short second in Ben's strong arms, inhaling the tired scent of the man, feeling the pleated wrinkles in the back of Ben's sweaty shirt, where he had been glued to the car seat for God knows how many hours.

Ben graciously pulled away, not abruptly, just... kindly. "Sorry it's such a terrible hour. I should have stayed at a motel tonight and finished driving in tomorrow, but I just couldn't make myself do it." He suddenly looked down at his own feet, embarrassed, then back to Paulie's face. "I've missed you, Paulie. It's really good to see you."

It was almost as if nothing had come between them. Paulie wondered if all the angst and paranoia and guilt he had been harboring for the past two years was centered only in his own head. My God, had Ben been so drunk he didn't remember that night at all? No, that was impossible. Why, then, would he have disappeared like he had?

"I've missed you too," Paulie said, feeling his heart accelerate at the words. The urge to apologize for that night was on the tip of his tongue, but he fought it. It was too soon.

Ben looked past him at the house, still dark at this early hour. Paulie hadn't switched on any lights on his way out the door. "Is everyone here? Jamie? Trevor?"

Paulie laughed. "And their boyfriends."

A flash of sadness crossed Ben's face. "I heard they weren't together."

"No," Paulie said, "but I have a feeling they might be by the time these next two weeks are over. If their lovers don't kill them first. Or they don't kill each other."

"Should be an interesting two weeks, then."

Paulie clutched Ben's arms, felt the hardness of his biceps beneath his shirtsleeves. He squeezed the firmness there and said, "I'm glad you made it. It'll be great to have us all together again."

"The four musketeers," Ben chuckled.

And Paulie joined him. "Yep. The four musketeers. Only now it's six—no, wait, seven. We have a houseboy for the next two weeks. He's a little, um, unusual."

Ben grinned. "Wouldn't expect anything less."

Paulie thought about explaining Jeffrey to him, then couldn't quite decide how he should do it. Finally, he decided he'd let Ben figure Jeffrey out on his own. Shouldn't take long.

Paulie pointed to the driveway entrance twenty feet over. He punched a button on the inside of the gateway where they were standing, and the wrought iron driveway gate slid open with a rumbling clank.

"Bring your car inside," Paulie said. "Park anywhere you want. Just not on my roses."

"Gotcha. Still doing the yard work, huh?"

"Yeah. I'm rich now, but I have to do *something.*"

"I had visions of you driving a little bulldozer around, moving your money from one pile to another like Scrooge McDuck."

"Oh, I do that too. Just not in front of company."

Ben laughed, and much to Paulie's surprise, Ben took his hand. "Come with me while I bring the car in, Paulie."

Pleased more than he would ever admit, even to himself, Paulie said, "Oh. Sure." Then he turned and whistled for Hammer. "Can't have you running over my dog. We'd better bring him with us."

Hammer came galloping around the corner of the house from somewhere in the back. He spotted Paulie by the gate and headed for him at a dead run, tongue flopping at one end, tail flopping at the other.

"Still a happy dog," Ben said.

"You have no idea."

Hammer took a minute to sniff at Ben's legs to say howdy, then leapt straight up into Paulie's arms. Paulie caught him with an "Oof!"

Ben's car was at the curb under a streetlight. Paulie took one look at it and blinked. It wasn't a car at all. It was a U-Haul moving van. A big one. On the side of the van was a huge painting of an extinct rhinoceros, which had apparently once resided in the suburbs of Omaha about ten million years ago. Maybe it had owned a condo there. An Audi station wagon was hitched to the back of the van, and a bicycle was clamped to the front bumper.

"Holy shit, Ben, you do know I only invited you for two weeks, right?"

Ben laughed. "I knew you'd say that. No, I'm moving back to the city. Left Omaha for good."

Paulie was stunned. "Oh. But what about your jo—?"

Ben rattled the keys in his hand. "Let's wait until we're in the house, then I'll tell you all about it. And don't worry, I won't be infringing on your hospitality any longer than the two weeks I was invited to infringe upon it."

That statement hurt. It really did. Paulie stopped and dragged Ben to a halt beside him. "You couldn't infringe on my hospitality if you tried. And if you need somewhere to stay while you're looking for a place of your own, then you can damn well stay here. Christ knows I've got the room. And it would be great to have you here. Plus, if you don't do it, I'll let all the air out of your tires, all *ten* of your tires—car, truck, and Cannondale—just to make *sure* you stay."

Ben considered that for a second with a wry grin on his face. Then he reached out and gave Hammer a chin rub. Paulie had the feeling he was doing it to kill time while he tried to figure out what to say.

All he finally *did* say was, "We'll see." But he looked appreciative when he said it.

Paulie happily took that appreciative look to mean yes. Actually he took it to mean *hell* yes.

He turned to the van and the car and the bike and apparently everything Ben owned in the world and said, "Well, let's get this stuff off the street before it drags down the property values. Then I'll show you to your room. You must be exhausted."

Ben shook his head. "Actually, I'm starving. You got anything to eat?"

Paulie beamed. "Sure. I'm hungry too. We'll have a nice cozy snack before the others get up. It may be the last quiet minutes we'll have together."

"I hope not," Ben said.

Paulie looked up sharply at the tone of sincerity in those three little words. His heart did another little tap dance inside his chest.

Before he could think of a response, Ben tugged him toward the van.

Still nestled in Paulie's arms, Hammer started wagging his tail, thinking they were going for a ride.

The eastern sky was just beginning to lighten with approaching dawn. A new day was beginning, and Paulie was suddenly wide awake.

ALONE IN the kitchen with Paulie, Ben displayed his first hint of shyness. To cover it he commented on the house. "You've kept the place exactly the way your grandmother had it. I can't see that you've changed a thing."

"I haven't," Paulie said. "I couldn't see much sense in changing it. Feels like home this way."

Ben cocked an eyebrow. A smile played at his mouth. "You didn't make a shrine out of your grandmother's bedroom, did you? You know, leaving everything the way it was, bed turned down, her robe hanging on the bedpost. Teeth in a glass on the nightstand. Pillows fluffed. All that."

Paulie laughed. "You mean like Norman Bates? No, Ben. I'm not that crazy. And I don't dress in her clothes either. Nor is she mummifying in the rocker by the window. And I seriously doubt if I'll slash you to ribbons with a butcher knife the first time you take a shower."

Ben gave a satisfied grunt, but there was a chuckle buried in it. "That's a relief."

"Although I did commandeer her room."

"Well, good. It was the best room in the house."

"No shit."

Paulie made himself busy dragging leftovers from dinner out of the fridge. He nuked a couple of things in the microwave to warm them up, then dumped it all on the counter where he and Ben pulled out a couple of stools and dug in. Ben really was hungry. He ate like it was his first good meal in a week.

Paulie enjoyed watching him eat. It was like they were back in their little apartment on the border of the San Diego State campus. Back where Paulie had spent what was probably the best year of his life.

Again, Paulie fought the urge to apologize for that long-ago night when everything changed. And once more, Paulie quelled the urge. *Not yet,* he told himself. *Not yet.*

Under the unforgiving fluorescent lights in the kitchen, Paulie got his first crystal-clear view of Ben since his arrival. The man was still as handsome as ever. Maybe even more handsome, or was that just Paulie's happiness talking? God, it was good to see Ben again. And the fact there seemed to be no residual side effects in Ben's mind from the night Paulie overstepped his boundaries made having Ben there even more enjoyable. If things kept going the way they were going, maybe Paulie would never have to apologize for that night at all. Although he knew he would. Someday, his own guilt would force the words out of him.

And it was only right he should. He knew that too.

Ben still wore his shock of black hair a little too long, a little unkempt, just as he had in college. It still hung in his eyes, and he was still pushing it back every two minutes to get it out of the way. Ben's brown eyes were still alive and darting, taking in the world around him with childlike hunger. Ben had always seemed to look at everything through a child's eyes—through a child's sensibilities. Except for that one drunken night when his adult persona had asserted itself and his sexuality exploded in Paulie's face (literally), leaving Paulie with a memory he hadn't been able to shake for the next two years.

Ben childlike was a joy. Ben sexual and eager and naked was mind-boggling.

Paulie shook that thought away, trying to head off the sudden renewal of craving he felt for his friend. His *best* friend. It was the exact same craving he had felt for Ben throughout his entire senior year at college, when they shared their little apartment together, and Paulie quickly realized the feeling was as intense now as it had been then. In fact, the intensity of his urge to drag Ben into his arms and make love to him right then and there was almost heart stopping. But he fought it.

Paulie had almost lost Ben's friendship once over his own weakness. He wouldn't let it happen again.

Paulie let the man eat for a few minutes before bombarding him with questions. It seemed the polite thing to do. But just when he decided he couldn't wait another minute to find out why Ben was moving back to the coast, Ben asked a question of his own. He asked it softly. Neither of them wanted to wake the others quite yet. They were enjoying their time alone.

"So Paulie, are you still writing?"

Paulie wasn't sure why his circulatory system decided to expend the effort, but all six quarts of his life's blood rushed straight to his face. Even his ears were suddenly burning. "Yeah. I'm still writing. For what it's worth."

"I'm sure it's worth a lot. Or one day will be."

Paulie shrugged, trying not to act embarrassed, but knowing he probably was. "I guess we'll find out. I just submitted a novel. My first. Mailed it off two days ago, in fact."

Ben dropped his fork with a clatter and lunged across the counter to give Paulie a hug. "That's great! It's what you always wanted!"

Paulie nodded, suddenly lost again in the feel of Ben's strong arms holding him tight, feeling the brush of Ben's five o'clock shadow grating against his own, smelling the heat of the man, closing his eyes to smell him even better. "I know. I'm finally living my dream. It will be a better dream if I'm ever actually published."

"Give it time," Ben said. "You will be. I don't doubt it for a minute."

Ben released him and sank back down on the stool to resume eating. His beautiful eyes were still flashing with happiness at what Paulie had told him. Paulie studied those eyes as he sat there, urging his heart to calm down. He was still a little breathless from the unexpected hug—the unexpected closeness. At the thrill of having Ben near after two years of missing him—after two years of wondering if they were still friends. And now that Ben was here, being almost delirious in the knowledge that he hadn't changed at all. Not one little bit.

Paulie had almost forgotten Ben's ability to make you feel like the most important person in the world, that the words you spoke were the most important words ever uttered. By *anybody*. It was one of the gifts, Paulie had always suspected, that would make Ben an excellent teacher.

"I want to read it," Ben said, again stuffing food in his mouth. There was a mischievous glint in his eye when he asked, "Got a print copy?"

Paulie smiled at that. Ben knew he was big on print copies. Always had been. "I do. Two, actually."

And Ben giggled. "Good old Paulie. Backup in case the Internet implodes. Right?"

"Something like that." He was blushing again.

"You always were a technophobe, Paulie."

Paulie threw his head back and laughed, blushing all the harder. He could feel it burning his cheeks. All three of his friends had constantly ragged him all the way through college about being a technophobe. And it was true. He was one then, and he was one now. Some things never change.

"You remembered."

Ben's broad smile ratcheted down a notch. But it was still a smile. It was still a knockout.

"You'd be surprised what I remember, Paulie."

Paulie's heart skidded to a stop. After a deafening moment of silence, it resumed beating. He wasn't ready for this. Not yet. It was too embarrassing. He steered the conversation to a safer heading. Away from himself. Away from what he'd done two years earlier. The mistake he'd made. That one stupid, life-changing mistake. If that was even what Ben was referring to. Maybe it wasn't, who knew? But Paulie couldn't take the chance. Not yet.

"What about *your* dream, Ben? What happened with your job in Omaha? Your teaching. What happened with that?"

Ben's face sobered. He looked down at Hammer, who was sitting on the floor by his chair, ever hopeful for another act of droppage; Hammer lived for droppage. So far he was being sorely disappointed. Neither Paulie nor Ben had dropped a goddamn thing.

Ben reached down to pat Hammer's head and said, "School cuts. Every school district in the country is short on money. When salaries need cutting, they go for the low man on the totem pole. That was me, of course. I knew it was going to happen. It's not like it came as a big surprise."

"I'm sorry," Paulie said, reaching out and patting Ben's hand.

Ben stared at Paulie's hand on his and made no move to slide his away. "I know you are. Thanks, Paulie." Then his face brightened. "But it's all for the better. I learned one very important fact in Omaha."

"And what was that?"

Ben laughed. "I'm allergic to corn pollen."

Paulie blinked. "Huh? What the hell is that supposed to mean?"

Ben's hand was still nestled comfortably under Paulie's. Both men were acutely aware of that fact, but neither did anything to change it. Ben's mind was elsewhere, maybe. But Paulie's wasn't. Paulie was savoring every moment of contact while he waited for Ben to respond—the feel of Ben's lean fingers pressing against the palm of Paulie's hand, the brush of the hair on the back of Ben's hand tickling Paulie's fingertips. Jesus. It was all Paulie could do not to lift Ben's hand and press it to his lips, to taste the man's flesh just one more time. Just for a second.

Finally, Ben answered, dragging Paulie's mind back to where it belonged. "Ever been to Nebraska in the summer, Paulie? Corn pollen is everywhere. Corn*fields* are everywhere. It came as news to me, but yours truly is allergic to that shit. I mean *allergic*. Never knew what a wuss I was until I hit America's heartland. So when the school district laid the bombshell on me that my contract would not be renewed for the following year, I actually jumped for joy. Don't get me wrong, I loved the teaching. The kids were great. Farm kids mostly. Wonderful, down-to-earth people. And their parents were great too. But I finally had to face the fact that I would be a much better teacher if I wasn't sneezing and blowing my nose every five seconds. And I lost ten pounds in Nebraska. I think it was mostly snot."

Paulie grinned. "So here you are."

Ben grinned right back. "Yep. Here I am. And glad of it. I've got a few leads on teaching positions here in the city, and I've still got the rest of the summer to hunt one down that I like. It should be okay. If not, I'll find some other kind of work until another school year starts. In the meantime, I'm glad to be back. San Diego will always be my home. Plus," he added shyly, "my best friend is here."

"Who's that?" Paulie asked.

And Ben snagged Paulie's fingers and twisted them back against his wrist. Playfully, but maybe not so playfully either.

"Uncle! Uncle!" Paulie screamed like a ten-year-old, and two seconds later, they were both roaring with laughter.

"Well, I'm glad you're here," Paulie said, after the laughter finally died down.

"Me too." Ben sounded like he meant it.

"I was going to plant a crop of corn in the backyard, but now I guess maybe I won't."

"Good. In that case I'll hang around for a while."

"Good," Paulie echoed, and that was that.

IT WASN'T surprising that Paulie had forgotten any romantic notions he might have harbored concerning his houseboy the minute Ben walked through his front door. Apparently, that only worked one way, though, because Jeffrey had most certainly not forgotten the romantic notions he had harbored about *Paulie.*

Paulie found this out when he glanced up from the counter where he and Ben were eating and laughing and saw Jeffrey standing in the doorway. He was in pajama bottoms that hung low on his hips, like they were just waiting for the guy to make the wrong move so they could plummet to the floor. A sprinkle of bristly pubic hair peeked above the waistband, and a sizable bulge swayed very enticingly beneath the loose fabric every time Jeffrey moved. If Ben hadn't been present, Paulie would undoubtedly have suffered a relapse as far as those previously considered romantic notions in regards to fucking around with the help were concerned.

Jeffrey gave Paulie a quizzical look. "Oh, there you are," he said. Then he added, "Sir."

Paulie stood as Ben turned toward the speaker as well. "Jeffrey. Did you need something?"

Paulie was all business, but by the surprised expression that crossed Jeffrey's face, and by the way his houseboy was dressed, or *half*-dressed, Paulie suspected he knew exactly what Jeffrey needed. And maybe he was looking up his boss to get a little of it when he stumbled upon him in the kitchen.

Jeffrey studied Ben and seemed to lose his resolve. "N-no. I just heard voices. Thought I'd check it out."

Paulie nodded. "Well, we're fine, Jeffrey. You can go on back to bed. The others probably won't be up for a while."

"Oh, okay then." Jeffrey cast another appraisal in Ben's direction, as if perhaps waiting for an introduction. By the time Paulie thought about giving him one, Jeffrey had already turned and disappeared.

Ben had a wicked smile on his face. "Houseboy?"

Paulie laughed. "Yeah. I couldn't find an ugly straight one."

"I'll bet."

They settled back down at the counter. Paulie poured them each another glass of milk.

While Ben picked at the food still left on his plate, Paulie could see the weariness settling over him. There were smudges under his eyes and a slight slump to his shoulders. With food in his stomach, he began to crave sleep. Paulie knew it even if Ben didn't.

Before he could think of a way to send Ben off to bed so he could get some rest before he collapsed, Ben raised his head away from his plate and centered somber eyes on Paulie's face. There was a world of memory reflected in their brown depths. And something more. Sadness, maybe. Paulie could see it there. His heart quickened as he waited for Ben to tell him what the memories were.

He didn't have to wait long.

"You look the same, Paulie. You haven't changed at all. I—I can't tell you how many times I sat in my apartment in Omaha and looked across the breakfast table at an empty chair wishing you were in it."

Paulie felt heat flare up behind his eyeballs, a precursor to tears. A sob threatened to climb from his throat. He forced a grin to his face to camouflage both feelings and groped through the rubble in his mind for something to say. What he finally settled on was a joke. Sort of.

"Don't they have women in Nebraska? I think I read somewhere they did. You could have had breakfast with one of them. The way you look, you could have had breakfast with a different one every morning."

Ben twisted his mouth into an awkward moue, bringing forth the dimple in his left cheek. A full-blown smile would have borne them both.

"I guess I was too busy to look," he said, glancing away uncomfortably. "Too busy and… too homesick. I'm a grown man, Paulie, but I never got over being homesick all the time I was there. Missing San Diego. Missing… people." Sadness dimmed Ben's eyes. Paulie watched as he stared through the kitchen window at the gray light of morning lighting the world outside. The stars had disappeared. The day was beginning.

Paulie wondered where the day would lead.

Ben's voice was soft. A library voice. It barely carried across the table.

"Take my hand, Paulie."

Hesitant and more than slightly confused, Paulie did as Ben asked. He stretched his arm across the table and laid his hand, palm up, in Ben's. He watched through still-burning eyes as Ben's fingers closed around it. Gently. Ben's thumb stroked the web of skin between Paulie's thumb and forefinger.

"I learned I need my friends around me, Paulie. I can't be happy if they're not there. I learned other things too, while I was gone. One of these days I'll tell you what they were. That okay?"

Paulie couldn't tear his eyes from Ben's thumb. Stroking. Stroking. The heat of it. The gentle strength. "Yes," he said. "You can tell me anything. You always could. I thought you knew that."

He finally raised his eyes to Ben's face. Their eyes connected for a brief moment before Ben once again turned his head to stare out the window. Embarrassed, maybe. Uncomfortable, certainly.

"I do know that," Ben said. And after a heartbeat of time, he added, "I've always known it. You're my best friend."

"And you're mine," Paulie answered.

They sat in the quiet kitchen listening to the clock on the wall as it ticked away the seconds.

"I need sleep," Ben finally said, squeezing the bridge of his nose.

And Paulie watched as their wonderful moment of connection flittered away into the ether.

He wondered if they would ever be lucky enough, or open enough, or *brave* enough, to find it again.

"Come on then," Paulie finally said, aching a little inside, missing Ben already. "Let's get you settled in your room before you fall flat on your face. I'll try to keep Trevor and Jamie from storming the castle gates or climbing up the trellis and crawling through your bedroom window when they find out you're here, but I can't promise anything. Those two are still pretty much as uncontrollable as they ever were."

Ben smiled a lazy smile and spoke around a yawn. "Good. I'm glad they haven't changed."

It was not by design that Paulie put Ben in the bedroom next to his. Not conscious design at any rate. Although it wasn't entirely accidental either, seeing as how they were the only two bedrooms in the mansion with connecting doors. The doors were lockable, of course, on either side, but still—there they were. Paulie had to admit there might have been a considerable amount of wishful thinking involved in putting Ben in that room. And even if neither of them ever set foot through the connecting door that separated their sleeping spaces, at least Paulie would know Ben was close. Perhaps he could even hear him snore, like he had in the old days, when Ben was sleeping just down the hall in their little apartment. That had been nice. Paulie had fallen asleep many nights with the gentle timbre of Ben's snoring comforting his thoughts—and tweaking his libido.

Ben had brought a suitcase in from the van with all his immediate needs inside. He flung it on the bed as Paulie closed the bedroom drapes so Ben could get some sleep. The California sun was rising quickly now, the world outside flooding with light. It would be another hot day.

Paulie stopped piddling around with the curtains when Ben said, "I'm glad I'm here, Paulie."

And Paulie nodded. "So am I."

Paulie turned from the window. He reached down and smoothed a wrinkle in the bedspread just because he had nothing better to do, and with a quiet "Get some rest," he headed toward the door.

Ben stepped into his path before he ever got there. Once again he folded Paulie into his arms.

"Thanks, Paulie. I'll see you later. Maybe we'll go for a jog. I'm stiff from being in that van for three days. A run would do me good."

Again, Paulie closed his eyes as he let Ben's warmth, Ben's touch, Ben's *presence,* radiate through him. He had to clear his throat to find his voice. "That would be great. I could use a good run myself."

He eased himself from Ben's arms, and Ben stood there, watching him move toward the door.

Just before he stepped over the threshold, Paulie said, "Sleep tight, Ben."

Ben smiled. "I will. And Paulie?"

Paulie stopped. "Yes?"

Ben's smile softened as he pushed his hair from his eyes. "You don't have to be afraid of me, you know. Whatever is in our past is part of who we are. It's what makes us friends."

"I—I know."

"I regret nothing," Ben said. "I don't want you to regret anything either."

Paulie's throat tightened. He opened his mouth to speak, but no sound came out. Desperately afraid of the tears threatening to reach his eyes, Paulie simply nodded.

He quietly closed the door between them.

Chapter 6

KNOWING HE would never sleep, Paulie headed back down to the kitchen, his mind a maelstrom of stampeding thoughts. Those thoughts were bouncing and ricocheting around inside his skull like shrapnel. How Ben looked. The things Ben had said. The feel of his embrace. His heat, his scent, his smile.

And that last comment. *I regret nothing,* he had said. What had Ben meant by that? Had he accepted what Paulie had pushed him into on that last night they spent together under the same roof? Accepted it and gone past it? Were Paulie's actions forgiven, if not forgotten?

Paulie shook his head to clear the cobwebs. Too much going on. Too much to try to think about at five o'clock in the morning.

His eyes popped open wide when he entered the kitchen. The mess he and Ben had left from their early morning eating spree only a few minutes earlier was now all cleaned up. Not a crumb in sight. Jeffrey must have snuck in and played house elf yet again while Paulie showed Ben his room.

Desperate to empty his head, Paulie looked around for something to do. The kitchen was spotless and glaringly bright under the fluorescent lights—all gleaming white walls, black-and-white tiled floor, stainless steel appliances. Paulie could see his own reflection staring back at him from a dozen polished surfaces. He decided to fill the coffee maker, then saw Jeffrey had already done it before he went to bed. He opened the dishwasher to put the dishes away. That was done too. Certain there must be something he could do, he stepped on the lever and popped the lid on the trash receptacle standing in the corner.

Spotless. Paulie was kind of surprised Jeffrey had turned out to be so damned efficient. Who knew the guy could look as sexy as he did and still end up being so competent at his job? In Paulie's experience, most people were usually proficient at either one or the other. Never both.

Since the coffee pot was ready to go, and since he owned the damn thing, Paulie made an executive decision and flipped the switch. Moments later the kitchen was filled with the delicious aroma of freshly brewing coffee. He suspected that would wake up the troops if nothing else would.

Turning, he suddenly realized one of the troops was already up. It was Danny. He was standing in the kitchen doorway. His hair was wild, his eyes puffy with sleep, he had a hickey on his neck that hadn't been there yesterday, and he was dressed in nothing but a baggy pair of swim trunks that reached all the way down to his knees. He looked cute as hell.

As he usually did, unless he was naked and cavorting in the pool with two other naked men, Danny seemed a little unsure of himself.

Paulie smiled, seeing through him in an instant. "You want the surfboard."

Danny nodded as a grin spread across his face. "If it's okay. I can hear the surf from our bedroom. I need to get out there in it. It's kind of a Zen thing with me."

Paulie laughed. "Of course it is." He pointed south. "Garage. The door's unlocked. There's a couple of surfboards standing in the corner. A shortboard and a longboard. Take your pick."

Danny grabbed three apples from a bowl and juggled them like a pro on his way out the door. He looked back at the last second with a sweet smile on his face. "Thanks."

"You're welcome. Don't drown."

"I won't, Mommy."

Paulie watched as Danny's smooth brown back and the humongous swimming trunks that clung to the delectable swell of his pale ass disappeared through the kitchen door. Paulie had just enough time to think how beautiful Danny was before the boy was gone.

With the coffee ready, Paulie poured himself a mugful and headed back to his room to clean up for the day. In the hall outside his bedroom door, he stopped and held his breath, listening. Sure enough, he could faintly hear the sound of Ben softly snoring. He was asleep already, exhausted from his long drive. Manhandling that bigass moving van cross-country with the station wagon dragging along behind wouldn't be a fun chore in anybody's reckoning. Paulie would hate to do it.

Ben wasn't really snoring loudly yet, but he was undoubtedly building himself up to it. He had always been a snorer. When Ben slept, he slept like he meant it. It was the same way he did everything. Unforgivingly all out. Determined. Unrelenting. Focused.

A tender smile turned Paulie's lips up at the memories the sound of Ben's snoring evoked. Memories of the apartment, the laughter in it, the friendship they shared.

And one odd memory too.

He remembered coming home from classes one day to find Ben in the living room on his knees next to his father, the minister. They were praying. At least Ben's *father* was praying, who knows for what. And while he prayed, with his hand clamped heavily on his son's shoulder like a vise to keep the boy on his knees beside him, Paulie saw that Ben's face was frozen in a rigor of embarrassment. When he glanced up and spotted Paulie, standing in the doorway watching them, his embarrassment turned to mortification. Not sure what was happening, and just as surely mortified for his friend as his friend was mortified for himself, Paulie eased his way back out the door and quietly closed it behind him.

Later, still shaking his head in horrified wonder, Ben told Paulie his father had shown up out of the blue and insisted on blessing the apartment.

Paulie asked for clarification. "You say he came to bless the apartment? You mean like… *pray for it?*"

Blushing again just thinking about it, Ben nodded. Both men gazed around at the apartment as if they were just now seeing it for the very first time. The place was a mess. It always was.

Paulie said what was on both their minds. "It would have been better if he'd come to clean."

"No shit," Ben agreed.

To Paulie, who didn't have a religious bone in his body, the fact that Mr. Martin felt the urge to pray over their crappy little apartment sounded strange indeed. Did the man think the joint was a den of immoral activity? Since Paulie had never kept his sexual preferences a secret, although he certainly hadn't flaunted them, either, was Reverend Martin worried about the ramifications of his son living under the same roof as a gay man? The man knew Trevor and Jamie too, and they never kept *anything* secret from *anybody*. In fact, they paraded their gayness every chance they got. Had Ben's dad grown unhappy that his son had gay friends? Did the good reverend think Paulie was leading his son down the slippery path to a burning eternity in hell? And now that he thought about it, Paulie would have been more than happy to do so, had Ben only asked. He thought he even knew exactly how to go about it. Heck, he could probably drag them both into hell without too much trouble. Lord knows he had imagined the perfect way to go about it enough times as he lay in bed beating off night after night after night to the memory of Ben strolling around the apartment naked.

Paulie chuckled now, thinking of that day. But that strange episode was only one of Paulie's memories.

Paulie remembered other things too. Things only Paulie would. The longing on Paulie's part. The lonely nights of touching himself to the sound of Ben's breathing in the other room. Ben, naked, making a sandwich at the kitchen counter as if Paulie wasn't even there, plopping his bare ass across from Paulie at the kitchen table. Shameless. Stunning. Perfect.

Paulie sipped his coffee as he shaved and showered and made himself presentable for the day. While he dressed, again in shorts and a T-shirt, he looked through his bedroom window at the haze of ocean stretching out from the rear of the property. Danny had been right. The surf was indeed up. He could hear it. The swells were huge, each and every one of them cresting magnificently in the glare of the rising sun slashing across the water. The breakers crashed landward in explosions of sound and spray, striking the rocks, booming like thunder. It was a surfer's wet dream. No wonder Danny wanted to be a part of it.

Paulie could see a handful of surfers even now, paddling out to meet the next swell, shiny, sleek bodies tense, preparing to leap to their feet atop their boards, daring the ocean to knock them off. Some in trunks, some in wetsuits. Each and every one of them playing chicken with the grand Pacific.

He spotted Danny on Paulie's own bright-yellow longboard, paddling like crazy, trying to reach the swell at just the right moment to catch a ride. Danny looked like he knew what he was doing. And he looked like he was having fun.

"It's kind of a Zen thing," Danny had said. And he was right. Surfing was a Zen thing indeed. Paulie agreed with the kid completely. But still, Paulie preferred running. That was a Zen thing too. And in Paulie's eyes, the ultimate Zen thing. It took skill and guts and practice to balance on a slab of fiberglass and ride a wave. It took more than skill and guts to run well. It took everything you had. Heart, soul, body, mind.

In fact, Paulie ached to get out there right now, head off down the beach to knock out a few miles in the sand. Sand running was always a tougher workout than street running. A whole new set of muscles came into play. Paulie longed for the exertion. He needed to clear his mind, test his body. He needed to reach that Zen place Danny had been talking about. That was the only place Paulie had ever found where he could totally disconnect, look at himself from a distance, and maybe understand his feelings a little better. And the only time Paulie had ever found that place was in the heart of a long run.

On any other day he would already be out there. Him and Hammer. A boy and his dog. Tearing up the beach. Having fun, vaulting sunbathers, splashing through the surf. Zenning like crazy. But not today. Today he would wait for Ben.

Ben. Paulie smiled just thinking the name. He could see the reflection of his smile in the windowpane in front of him. Then he watched himself give a little mocking headshake at that damned reflection.

He was still nuts about Ben. That's what the confusion in his mind all boiled down to. The past two years hadn't dimmed his attraction for Ben one teeny iota. If anything, it seemed to have intensified it. Jesus, would he never learn? Surely, every gay man on the planet had enough sense not to fall for a straight guy. Every gay man but him at any rate. What a sap he was.

Paulie clucked his tongue at himself as he looked through his reflection to stare out at the ocean again, feeling a little burst of vicarious endorphins rage through his system as he watched Danny ride the curl. Graceful. Relaxed. Competent. The kid was good. In fact, he was better than Paulie.

Paulie smiled, watching him go. Then he laughed out loud when Danny took a tumble backward off the board.

He continued to watch until he saw Danny's head pop safely out of the water. He was thankful too that the kid had had the good sense to tether himself to Paulie's longboard. Paulie would hate to lose that board. He had owned it since high school. A gift from his grandmother. It was the best he'd ever ridden.

As soon as he knew for sure that both the kid and the board were safe, Paulie turned from the window and prepared to begin his day.

But before any beginning actually got underway, he stood in the middle of the room and stared at the connecting door to Ben's room.

Had Ben locked his side of the door? Without twisting the knob, Paulie had no way of knowing. Paulie had not locked his own side. He knew that without a doubt because he had checked it countless times during the past couple of days while he waited for Ben to arrive. In fact, as soon as he had decided to put Ben in that room, the door checking had begun. Two or three times a day. First one side, then the other. And for what? Did he really think Ben would come sneaking through that door one night, as hungry for Paulie as Paulie was hungry for him? God, he was pathetic.

Paulie closed his eyes and listened. Ben's snoring was louder now. Paulie smiled. He loved that sound. Pretty soon the guy would be rattling the blinds, his mighty snore sucking the light bulbs right out of the sockets. He imagined Ben's sleep-warm body sprawled naked under the sheet, his hot, clean breath warming the pillow, his too-long hair splayed haphazardly across his face. Simply imagining how Ben would look in his sleep, how he would smell, how he would feel, caused Paulie's dick to press against the fabric of his shorts. Waking up. Looking around. Wondering what all the hubbub was about. Hoping for a little action.

"Down, boy," Paulie mumbled to his own crotch. And how insane was that? Talking to one's body parts.

A soft tapping at his door disturbed Paulie's amorous thoughts.

It was Jeffrey, he supposed, playing it to the hilt again, offering a morning coffee, or a croissant, or a blowjob. A houseboy on a mission. It said a lot about Paulie's frame of mind that he actually considered accepting one, and he wasn't talking about a croissant. Although deep down he knew he really wouldn't. Not with Ben in the house.

Paulie swung open the door even while he tugged the tail of his T-shirt down to cover his expanding crotch. No sense egging the guy on.

He poked his head out into the hall and was surprised to see it wasn't Jeffrey standing there at all. It was Jack. Jamie's Jack. The hairdresser. He was dressed in a nightshirt that barely covered his junk. The nightshirt had a picture of a cat on the front of it. Geez, the guy even slept nelly. Although Paulie had to admit the bare legs poking out from beneath that silly nightshirt were very attractive indeed, if you liked hairless men. Which Paulie really didn't.

"Oh, hi," Paulie said. "Did you need something?"

The act of Paulie dragging the tail of his shirt over his crotch wasn't lost on Jack. He tore his eyes away from the movement with considerable difficulty, or so it seemed to Paulie. He supposed he should take that as a compliment.

Jack leaned against the doorframe, his hand against the wood at about head level, which dragged his nightshirt up to just a fraction of an inch above propriety's standard. In other words, his balls were showing.

Paulie tried to ignore them.

"I woke up alone," Jack said, his eyes still traveling back and forth between Paulie's crotch and his face. "Wondered if maybe you knew where Jamie had gone."

Paulie shrugged. "Haven't seen him. Maybe he went for a walk. It's a beautiful morning."

Jack didn't seem to be interested in a weather update. He again dropped his eyes to Paulie's crotch, and this time Paulie got a little annoyed about it. Christ, hadn't the guy ever heard of being monogamous? No? How about faithful? Did that ring a bell?

Paulie squeezed past Jack into the hall, just in case the guy took it into his head to make a move on him. He didn't trust that look of lust in Jack's eyes. Wow, and Paulie thought *he* was a slut.

"I love your house," Jack said, stepping aside to let Paulie pass but not stepping *away,* still lounging in Paulie's zone. Still standing too close. "You must be really rich."

"Uh, well…."

Jack edged a wee bit closer. "I mean, nothing wrong with being rich, right? Some people might even find that a very attractive asset in a man."

"Oh gee, I don't—"

"Jamie and I both appreciate you having us here. Anytime I can do anything to show my gratitude, just let me know."

"Well, uh, gee, uh—you and *Jamie* are welcome here anytime. As long as you and *Jamie* are an *item,* just think of my house as your house. As long as *Jamie's* there *too,* of course. Hehehe."

Jack batted his eyelashes. Paulie had never really seen a man do that before. "Well, it's not like we're actually joined at the hip, Jamie and me. We still enjoy a certain amount of freedom to see other people."

"Uh huh. That's nice."

Paulie was just beginning to wonder how to get rid of the guy, who he suspected was about to show his true colors—that of a cheating, gold-digging prick—when they both heard a sound from down the hall. A thumping sound. In fact a *lot* of thumping sounds. The noise was coming from Trevor's room. It reminded Paulie of Ricky Ricardo going apeshit with his bongos.

Jack leered. "Unless the Harlem Globetrotters are down there dribbling basketballs all over the place, that sounds like a headboard banging against a bedroom wall. Guess Trevor and the sixth grader are having a morning fuck. Sounds like a good one too."

Paulie looked behind him through his own bedroom door and out past the window to the ocean beyond—the ocean where Trevor's boyfriend was currently riding the waves. If Danny was actually having a morning fuck at the moment, Paulie didn't know how the hell he was managing it, unless he was fucking a dolphin.

Paulie dragged his eyes back into the hall when he heard footsteps coming up the stairs. Soon Jeffrey's handsome head appeared above the top stair. Then his broad shoulders came into view, and the tray he held in his hands containing a coffee pot and a stack of cups and saucers. He was about to serve coffee to the boss and his guests.

Paulie again looked toward Trevor's bedroom door, behind which the headboard banging was reaching a crescendo. If it was Tchaikovsky's *1812 Overture*, they would be firing the cannons about now.

Paulie had to think about this. If Trevor was partaking of a morning fuck, and if Danny was out surfing, and if Jack was standing in Paulie's doorway trying to look enticing, and if Jeffrey was climbing the stairs with a tray of coffee cups—then who the hell was Trevor fucking?

There was only one possibility, and even an idiot could figure it out.

Jamie. Who else? Seems Trevor and Jamie were taking a stroll (or a fuck) down memory lane.

Again.

Great.

In hopes of heading off World War III, Paulie took Jack's arm and steered him toward the stairs. Jeffrey saw them coming and seemed to be fairly astounded by the fact that Jack's nightshirt had been dragged up even higher by the way Paulie had clutched the man's arm. He didn't seem to be upset by it, though. He seemed to be *fascinated*.

Paulie said, "Jeffrey, take our friend downstairs and pour him some coffee. No need to serve our guests room to room. They'll be along shortly. You can serve them all in the kitchen when they get there."

Behind Jack's back, Paulie rolled his eyes up into his head to draw Jeffrey's attention to the headboard banging down the hall. Being a slut in his own right, Jeffrey got the drift of what Paulie was trying to tell him immediately.

He balanced the tray in one of his broad, capable hands, and with the other hand took control of Jack's arm, which Paulie relinquished to him with the skill of a relay runner passing the baton.

Jack seemed a little stunned by the fact that first Paulie, and now Jeffrey, were trying to hustle him down the stairs, but when Jeffrey scooped his long muscular arm around Jack's shoulder and in the process dragged his nightshirt up even higher, Jack apparently decided not to fight the inevitable. In fact, he was once again eyeing Jeffrey's towering mass of Nubian manhood with considerable appreciation, just as he had the day before in the pool, although at the moment, Jeffrey just happened to be fully dressed. The same certainly could not be said for Jack. His nightshirt was up around his armpits by now, leaving absolutely nothing below the man's clavicles to anyone's imagination.

Paulie wondered how long either of them would stay dressed once they reached the kitchen and found themselves fortuitously alone. He could hear them already giggling at the foot of the stairs.

Christ, he hoped they wouldn't fuck on the butcher-block table. Paulie would never be able to chop vegetables on it again. He'd have to chuck it and buy a new one.

While Paulie was still worrying about body fluids splattering across his butcher-block table, he heard a most horrendous moan coming through the door of Trevor's bedroom. Then he heard a second horrendous moan, this one in a different timbre. Obviously, whatever was taking place behind Trevor's bedroom door involved two men. Two *excited* men. The headboard of Trevor's bed banged against the wall in a frenzied flurry of thuds, sounding rather like a jackhammer tearing up a street, and then, after one mind-jarring, god-awful crash—which Paulie suspected was the fat ceramic lamp on the nightstand hitting the floor and smashing to smithereens—he heard nothing. Dead silence.

Wow, Paulie thought. *That was a porno-quality, tandem orgasm if I ever heard one. Those guys really do belong together.*

Then Paulie thought maybe he could find a store that carried table lamps *and* butcher-block tables. Save some running around.

A moment later, Trevor's door creaked open and a head peeked out. It was Jamie, looking the other way. He stepped out into the hall stark naked and started tugging on a pair of pajama bottoms, hopping around on one foot as he did it.

He turned and noticed Paulie, who was grinning at him from two doors down. Jamie's hair was sticking straight up off the top of his head, and his cheeks and ears were brick red.

"Nice afterglow." Paulie grinned. "Also, you have a dollop of semen in your hair."

"Oh, thanks," Jamie said, running his fingers through his hair to spread the semen around like Butch Wax. It was a pretty good dollop. It left his bangs standing straight up off his forehead like a picket fence. "Seen Jack?"

Paulie tapped a fingertip on his chin and gazed up at the ceiling. "Jack. Jack. Oh, you mean the man you came with. I don't mean just now, of course. I mean the man you came to the *mansion* with."

Trevor poked his head through the door behind Jamie. He pulled Jamie into him and planted a kiss on his mouth. When he was finished, he looked down the hall and spotted Paulie.

"Good morning," Trevor said with a broad, beaming smile. His cheeks were rosy too. But not brick red like Jamie's. More like wet, steaming terra cotta. "What's up?"

"Oh, nothing." Paulie smiled back, all innocence and good cheer. "What's up with you, sunshine?"

Trevor stepped out into the hall and stood behind Jamie because he was naked. "We had a bit of an accident. Please tell me the table lamp on the nightstand wasn't from the Ming Dynasty. It seems to have suffered a fatal accident."

Paulie grunted. "Don't worry. It was just a rip-off. It's really hard to find a bona fide Ming Dynasty table lamp."

"Oh, good," said Jamie and Trevor in unison.

A worried look crossed Trevor's face, even while he reached his arms around Jamie and began manipulating Jamie's nipples from behind. "Seen Danny?"

"Stop that," Paulie said. "And yes. I've seen both your boyfriends. Danny is out surfing, and Jack is downstairs flirting with the help. At least I hope he's still flirting."

"That boy is such a slut," Jamie said.

"I've been meaning to talk to you about that," Trevor said. He was still twiddling Jamie's nipples, and now he was also nibbling at Jamie's neck from behind.

Paulie tried not to laugh. "You are both fine ones to talk." He was also getting a little turned on, watching a naked Trevor nibbling at Jamie's neck, while something seemed to be tentpoling the front of Jamie's pajama bottoms. Apparently the man had remarkable recuperative powers. Who knew?

Then both Trevor and Jamie froze. With Trevor still gnawing at Jamie's neck and Jamie still reaching around behind to grope through Trevor's hair, they both cocked their heads to the side and listened.

Finally, Trevor spoke. "What's that noise? A buzz saw?"

"Sounds more like a gnu gargling," Jamie said.

Trevor giggled. "You mean gnargling."

They slowly focused their attention on the door next to Paulie's bedroom. Their still-flushed faces lit up like stoplights.

"Benny!" Trevor screamed.

"The preacher's boy is here!" That was Jamie.

Paulie tried to wave them to silence, which he figured was sort of like trying to stop a couple of ICBMs with a Wiffle bat. And he was right. It didn't work at all.

He was horrified to see them ignore him completely and head straight for Ben's bedroom door. He was horrified because Trevor was still as naked as a jaybird. And sporting a hard-on to boot. Hell, they both were. Paulie was pretty sure Ben wouldn't want to wake up to *that.*

Paulie managed to scramble to the door in front of them and spread his arms wide to bar the way, but it was a close call. He could still hear Ben snoring away like a wood chipper behind him, thank God.

He lowered his voice accordingly. "You guys get dressed before your boyfriends catch you fondling each other. Ben will get up when he's good and ready. And Jesus, Jamie, go wash the come out of your hair."

Trevor leaned in close to examine Jamie's head. "Oh, so *that's* what that is. An errant shot. Sorry."

Jamie reached down and cupped Trevor's hard-on. "Maybe if we practice, your aim will improve."

Trevor snuggled closer to his ex. "Hmm. Maybe it will."

Once again, Paulie was getting horny watching those two. Horny and annoyed.

He rolled his eyes skyward as he pushed both men down the hall, being none too gentle about it. "Well, practice somewhere else. Go. Clean up. Jeffrey will be serving breakfast in the kitchen. Jack is already down there."

"*That* slut," Jamie said.

"Pot calling the kettle black," Paulie grumped, standing his ground until the two took the hint and finally set off down the hall under their own steam.

Before they entered Trevor's bedroom, he heard Jamie say, "Paulie's turned into a real prissy puss, don't you think?"

"I do indeed," Trevor agreed. "He's rich, though. That makes up for it."

"You bet it does," Jamie said. "I love the armoire in my room. Wonder if I can sneak it out of the house when we leave?"

"We can try."

The last thing Paulie saw was Trevor politely motioning Jamie through the doorway first, a kindness Jamie accepted like a gentleman. As he stepped into the room, Jamie circled Trevor's stiff cock with his fist and dragged Trevor through the door behind him.

When the door closed with a click, Paulie collapsed against the wall and breathed a sigh of relief. Then he stopped breathing long enough to listen.

Ben was *still* snoring. Jeez, that guy could sleep through anything.

Chapter 7

IT WAS well past noon before Ben ventured from his bedroom. By that time, breakfast was long over and Paulie's guests were once again lounging by the pool and soaking up alcohol like a bunch of drunken sponges. Paulie was nursing an apple juice, not wanting to drink alcohol since he and Ben had a running date later. He also couldn't help remembering the trouble he had caused the *last* time he got drunk with Ben around.

As the morning advanced, Paulie had grown ever more astounded by all the changes in the group dynamic which had taken place since the night before. He continually shook his head in wonder at the calm demeanor of his guests as they regrouped, reorganized, and reprioritized their canoodling arrangements.

Jamie and Trevor were still hanging onto each other with blissful abandon, no longer caring who saw them, if they ever did. Paulie was glad to see it, of course; he was sorry they had ever broken up with each other to begin with, but still he was amazed by the reactions of the two men Jamie and Trevor originally flew into town with.

Jack didn't seem to mind at all that Jamie was now focused entirely on his ex. Paulie figured this was primarily because Jack was now focused entirely on Jeffrey. Jack, it seemed, had a special place in his heart for big, tall, handsome black men with huge dicks. Or maybe that special place he had for big, tall, handsome black men with huge dicks wasn't his heart at all. Maybe it was more like his ass. Paulie suspected this not only because of the self-satisfied simper that now seemed firmly planted on Jack's face, but also because, in Paulie's opinion at least, the guy was definitely walking funny. Funny like maybe he had just sat on a fence post or some other long, solid, quivering object.

Whatever the case, Paulie was pretty sure some sort of sexual activity had already taken place between Jeffrey and Jack. They couldn't have been long about it, only having a very short window of time between when Paulie hustled Jack down the stairs with Jeffrey and when Paulie strolled into the kitchen barely fifteen minutes later. But Paulie could hardly blame Jack for being infatuated. Jeffrey really was a stunner. And the fact that both men had all the morals of a couple of goats didn't slow things down much either. Paulie feared that with Jack continually hanging all over his new houseboy, the domestic service might begin to suffer. But it hadn't yet. And Paulie figured even deteriorating domestic service was preferable to jealous wailing and scenes of teeth-gnashing drama between warring boyfriends. Paulie wasn't a big fan of angst.

At the moment, Jack and Jeffrey were lounging in deck chairs, dressed in swimming trunks for a change, and sipping at beers on the far side of the pool while they shared a huge bowl of buttered popcorn. Hammer sat expectantly between them and caught the occasional offering of a popcorn kernel tossed his way. His tail was sweeping the pool apron behind him. One happy dog.

If either Jack or Jeffrey cared that Jack's boyfriend and his boyfriend's ex and his ex's *new* boyfriend were cuddling in six feet of water in front of them, they certainly didn't show it.

For that, Paulie was extremely thankful. He liked things congenial.

Danny, the other new boyfriend, apparently liked things congenial as well. He didn't seem to mind at all that his main squeeze, Trevor, was now harboring less than chaste thoughts about his ex. In fact, Danny seemed to share the problem. The three were now a unit. Paulie sat by the pool watching them with no small amount of fascination. They were in the water, naked again, hanging on the edge of the pool, Jamie, Trevor, and Danny, their arms around each other, all six legs intertwined, kissing, smooching, carrying on, and not giving a rat's ass who watched them.

Danny was a free spirit, no doubt about that. And Paulie had to admit to himself that he was a wee bit jealous of his two friends. He had a feeling their night ahead, with Danny eager and gorgeous in bed between them, was going to be a golden ticket event. He wouldn't mind attending the festivities himself.

At the sound of bare feet pattering across the wooden deck at his back, Paulie turned and his heart gave a lurch when he saw Ben approaching. He had finally woken and decided to join the party. As he strolled across the patio in his lemon-yellow Speedos, heading for the pool and waving a cheerful hello to Jamie and Trevor, Paulie forgot about everything else. Jack, Danny, Trevor, Jamie, Jeffrey. Even Hammer. All five men and the dog slipped into a crevice in Paulie's brain and disappeared without a gurgle.

My God. Ben was still the most beautiful man Paulie had ever seen in his life.

Just as long and lanky as he had been in college, Ben now sported less of a tan than he had then, thanks no doubt to the Nebraska winters. But while his skin was paler, it still shone with health. And somehow, without the tan he was even more beautiful. The muscle definition was cleaner. The thick dark hair on his well-muscled legs and the thin trail of hair leading down from his navel to burrow its way inside the crotch of his Speedos were even more pronounced. There was a sprinkling of freckles across Ben's shoulders that had been hidden beneath a tan. And his chest was no longer completely smooth: at some time during the past two years, a small patch of chest hair had sprouted dead center between Ben's luscious brown nipples and neatly delineated pecs.

Ben's arms and hands were just as Paulie remembered them. Strong, well veined, competent looking. There was a grace to the movement of Ben's sturdy fingers that had always drawn Paulie's eye every time the man made a gesture with them. Ben's lean, expressive hands, Paulie thought, were the perfect accompaniment to the grace of Ben's perfectly sculpted body.

Paulie would never have thought it possible, but in the two years since Paulie had last seen him, Ben had become even more stunning than he had been in college. More confident. It was as if he had grown into himself. As if he had finally settled on who he was going to be.

But Ben's smile was the same as ever. Dimpled, sexy, sweet. At the moment he was flashing that smile at full wattage as he eyed everyone around the pool. First Paulie, then Jamie and Trevor. And finally even offering a shy acknowledgment to the strangers staring at him. Jeffrey, Jack, Danny.

And they *were* staring, Paulie noticed. Jeffrey and Jack looked like a couple of sugar addicts eyeing a stack of donuts as they took in Ben's sexy frame and tiny yellow Speedos. Danny appeared to appreciate the beauty of the new arrival too, but he still draped his arms around the two men beside him. He merely nodded and waved and laughed as Jamie and Trevor went totally batshit.

"The straight boy's up!" Trevor cried. "And damn, he's looking *good.*"

Jamie chimed in with, "Get your pale ass over here and give us a hug, you cornhusking nitwit!"

Ben laughed and strode to the edge of the pool where he bent down and awkwardly gave Trevor and Jamie a hug. Danny was included in the hug too, since he was ensconced between the two.

Trevor didn't seem to think he was getting his money's worth with the hug so he grabbed Ben's arm and dragged him into the pool headfirst. They all submerged and came up sputtering and whooping and horsing around.

Once in the water, Ben did his best to give them the kind of hug they wanted. If he was leery of the fact his old friends were naked beneath the water, he didn't make a big deal of it. He hugged, laughed, joked, and even gave Danny another hug. At that point Trevor and Jamie bellowed in mock outrage and pushed Ben away.

"The little one's ours!" Trevor teased. "You want a cute surfer dude, go find your own."

Ben laughed and blushed, his eyes glancing up to Paulie, who was watching from the lounge chair. Then he blushed even redder when he saw Paulie laughing with the rest.

Paulie took pity on him and reached over the water to give Ben a boost out. Ben rose like a phoenix: sputtering, splashing, the pool water sluicing smoothly through his dark body hair, laying it flat against his legs and stomach. His thick head of hair was slathered on his cheeks, and the slathering made him look about twelve years old. Paulie tried not to stare at the bulge in the little yellow Speedos as he handed Ben a towel to dry his hair.

Still laughing and dripping, Ben plopped himself down on the lounge chair next to Paulie's, and gave a wave to Jack and Jeffrey, who were still staring hungrily at him from across the pool.

They were so smitten, they looked like zombies. It actually took them a second to raise their hands and return a robotic wave.

Paulie thought that was about the funniest thing he'd ever seen.

Ben merely blushed again.

Reaching out his hand, Ben gave Paulie's blond hair a good-natured tousle, then he laid back on the chaise lounge and continued to run the towel over his body, drying himself off.

Two seconds later, Jeffrey was at Ben's side, bending down in his baggy swim trunks, his gorgeous tall body eclipsing the sun, and asking Ben very politely if he would care to partake of a cocktail, since the bar was indeed fucking open. (Jeffrey's words.)

"Holy crap," Ben said, trailing his eyes all the way up Jeffrey's six-foot-six frame to that handsome black face looming on high. He blinked against the glare of what appeared to be three hundred shiny white teeth glistening down at him.

Jeffrey smiled benignly. "Sorry, Boss. We're all out of holy crap. How about a beer?"

Taken by surprise, Ben glanced at Paulie before answering. He obviously wasn't used to being waited on with such fawning devotion to duty. Especially by a towering Adonis with muscles all over the place and a bulge in the crotch of his trunks that would have scared *anybody* to death.

Paulie laughed. "Don't worry. Just play along." To Jeffrey, Paulie said, "Why don't you just bring us a couple of Cokes. And stop trying to be so intimidating."

"Yes sah, massa!" Jeffrey saluted, all smiles. "Two Cokes it is! And hold the intimidation. Yes, sah!"

He hustled off to the cabana. Tall, stunning, sexy. Every eye around the pool watched him go.

Ben blinked and gave Paulie a questioning look. "Massa?"

Paulie shook his head. "He's being funny. Don't worry, he doesn't have one drop of slavish humility rooting through his system. He's far too proud for that. And smart. In fact, he's a biology major, working his way through Beaumont. Good houseboy though, when he isn't banging the guests."

Paulie glanced over at Jack on the other side of the pool, and Ben followed where he was looking.

Jack had that sugar-addict expression on his face again, only this time he seemed to be craving *brown* sugar, since he was watching Jeffrey gracefully skirt the pool and head off into the cabana on his long, dark, beautiful legs.

Ben's smile went on high beams again. "I see," he said.

Trevor and Jamie were resting their heads on their folded arms as they looked up at Ben from the edge of the pool, where they were drifting in the water. Danny was submerged between the two men doing God-knows-what to either one or both of them. Paulie was glad the edge of the pool kept Ben from seeing exactly what Danny was up to down there, although he himself wouldn't have minded a glimpse or two.

Considering the fact that a handsome young man was doing what appeared to be an underwater survey of his naked crotch, Trevor sounded amazingly nonchalant. "There's a U-Haul truck parked at the side of Paulette Manor, Benjamin, and seeing as how *we* didn't put it there, we figure it must be yours. Either you seriously overpacked for a two-week visit, or something's going on. Explain."

Ben rose up onto his elbows and gazed down at the two at his feet. "Moving back to town. Paulie knows about it. Lost my teaching job due to budget cuts, and now I'm looking for a position here. And speaking of positions, I fear your little friend is going to drown soon if he doesn't come up for air."

Trevor grinned. "He'll be all right. He's snorkeling. Although I don't know how much oxygen he's going to get out of that thing he's snorkeling. Might get something else, though."

Jamie jumped. "Oops! Now he's snorkeling me! What a lovely lad!"

Ben laughed and turned away to center his gaze on Paulie. "Haven't changed much, have they?"

"I'm afraid you're mistaken," Paulie groused. "They're actually worse."

Trevor eyed his two friends lying on their lounge chairs at the edge of the pool. Paulie suspected he was wondering what exactly was going on between Paulie and Ben. He also had a clever glint in his eye that hinted that perhaps he knew *exactly* what was going on between them. Or between *one* of them at any rate. Paulie's look of lust every time he centered his attention on Ben made that much crystal clear.

"So," Trevor said to Ben. "Missed California, did you?"

Ben was digging a finger in his ear, trying to get the water out. "Missed it like crazy," he said. "Missed all you guys. Plus I had some unfinished business to attend to in San Diego."

"Oh, really," Trevor said. "Unfinished business, huh?"

"Yes." Ben stared unflinchingly at Trevor's face, almost as if he was afraid to look anywhere else.

Ben was starting to blush again. In fact, so was Jamie, hanging at the edge of the pool by Trevor's side. He was getting that brick-red look to his face that he had had in the hallway earlier. What the hell was Danny doing underneath the water? And when the hell was he going to come up for air?

The final question was answered when Danny suddenly burst from the water. He sucked in a great gulp of air, laughing and sputtering and coughing while he did it.

He got his bearings and resumed his place between Jamie and Trevor, arms spread wide, dragging both men into another cuddle.

"Thank you, son," Jamie cooed in Danny's ear. "If that was a coming attraction, I can't wait for the major event."

"Coming attraction indeed." Trevor giggled. "Coming all over the place."

"More than likely," Jamie commented. "If the lad hadn't run out of air, I would have shown him what coming was all about."

Danny seemed to find that funny. "Big talk, old man."

Again, Ben rubbed the towel through his hair, probably to hide his embarrassment, and at that moment Jeffrey returned with two glasses of Coke in big plastic tumblers with ice and straws and lime wedges floating on the top.

He handed one to Ben, one to Paulie, then rather than skirt the pool again, dove over the three sluts at his feet and swam to the far edge before hoisting himself out, pulling up the back of his trunks, which had damn near slid off in the dive, and plopping himself down beside Jack again, who seemed more than happy to have him back. Two seconds later they were schmoozing and feeding each other popcorn while Hammer lay at their feet praying for another donation.

"So you've moved back for good, then," Trevor said to Ben, while Danny nibbled first at his neck, then at Jamie's.

"I hope so." Ben smiled, finally seeming to overcome his embarrassment as he watched Danny in action. Danny was chowing down on the two men at either side of him like a starving party guest ensconced between two trays of hors d'oeuvres and devouring both.

Lord, Paulie thought, *Danny's so cute even a straight guy finds him fascinating.*

Then Paulie saw that Ben was actually getting a little embarrassed after all. He directed his words in Paulie's direction for a change, like maybe he didn't want to be caught staring at the goings on in the water.

"It depends on the job market here for schoolteachers, of course. But hell, it has to be better than the market in Nebraska, right? And like I said last night, if I have to take a different type of job until another school year begins, then that's what I'll do. I'm not proud. Work is work. Although I'd rather teach if I can."

"Don't worry," Paulie said, studiously ignoring the three in the pool. "You'll find something. I'm sure of it."

Paulie turned away from Ben and spoke to Trevor. He would have spoken to Jamie too, but Jamie had disappeared. Now *he* was underwater and *Danny* was turning brick red. It didn't take a Rhodes scholar to figure out what was going on.

"Ben's going to stay here with me until he finds a place of his own," Paulie said.

Trevor seemed to find that extremely interesting. He gazed first at Paulie, then at Ben, then back to Paulie again. "Oh, really. And isn't it sweet of Paulie to offer?"

"Yes," Ben glowered. "It is. And wipe that smirky-ass smirk off your face."

At that moment Danny craned his head back and gave a keening wail. The tendons in his neck stood out, and he grabbed at Trevor's hair like a Titanic survivor snatching a life preserver. Trevor yelled, "Yeouch!" Then one look at Danny's face told him what was going on. He grinned and stuck his tongue in Danny's ear while Danny gasped—then gasped again.

"Oh Jesus!" Danny cried. "Oh Jesus!"

Five seconds later, Jamie exploded from the water in front of them, all smiles. "Damn," he said, sucking in air and wiping his mouth with the back of his hand. "That was delicious." He pressed his lips to Danny's throat while Trevor continued to nibble at the side of Danny's neck. The boy was trembling in the water. In fact, all three of them were trembling in the water.

Trying to head off a hard-on, Paulie leapt to his feet and dragged Ben up with him.

"Let's go for a run," he all but begged.

Ben nodded, as eager as Paulie to get away. "Maybe we should. It'll give them time to throw a few chemicals in the pool."

Paulie laughed. Although a truckload of germ-gobbling chemicals probably wouldn't be a bad idea.

PAULIE WAS dressed in running shorts, ankle socks, and his favorite running shoes. He had a bandanna knotted around his neck to catch the sweat.

Ben, after rummaging through the U-Haul truck for ten minutes to find his battered Asics, had finally joined him. He wore running shorts as well, and a raggedy muscle shirt that looked like it had been hemmed with a pocketknife and only came down to just above his belly button.

To Paulie's surprise, Ben gave Paulie's body an appreciative once-over. "You've stayed in shape," he said shyly.

"You too," Paulie said, trying to sound casual but probably failing miserably. Calling Ben "in shape" was a little like calling the *Mona Lisa* "a nice picture." It didn't do the artwork justice by any means.

"Street or sand?" Paulie asked, dragging his eyes back to Ben's face.

"Sand, if it's okay," Ben answered. "I've missed the ocean."

"Sand it is."

They left the mansion and skirted the pool, ignoring a chorus of wolf whistles and hoots from the morons still in attendance there, and headed for the redwood staircase leading down from the property to the beach.

It was still early afternoon. The sun was at its highest and hottest. Paulie loved the heat of it on his skin, and his heart was racing already. He loved to run. And he had always loved running with Ben. Back in college they ran almost every weekend. Even participated in a few marathons together.

After a few hamstring stretches to limber up and a good shake to get the blood moving, they set a leisurely pace up the beach, heading north, breathing in the sea air and letting their strong legs adjust to the pull of the sand in their treads. Down here, a breeze came off the water that had not been felt up at the house. The breeze was warm and silky against Paulie's skin—the air alive with that fishy, homey smell of saltwater and sea life.

The ocean cast foaming breakers across the sand every few seconds, but Paulie and Ben stayed far enough up on the beach to keep their trainers dry. There is nothing worse than running in wet shoes.

There were sunbathers and kids scattered around, but not many. This part of the La Jolla coastline was a little too far off the beaten path for the tourists to have found the place yet. Here the sun worshippers were mostly locals. Paulie even recognized a few, nodding or waving now and then as he passed them sprawled out on the sand, slathered in lotion, reading, basking, turning brown, looking like they owned the world; and if they could afford to live in this neighborhood, they damn near did.

It only took a few hundred yards for Paulie to realize how much he had missed running with Ben. They quickly reverted to that comfortable camaraderie they had always experienced when jogging together, and since they were very nearly the same height, their strides matched almost perfectly. It made for an easy, comforting workout—never having to adjust your stride to someone else.

They chatted as they loped along. Paulie was thrilled to see the happiness on Ben's face as he stared lovingly out at the ocean. Sometimes, Paulie would lag a few steps back just to soak up the sight of Ben's strong back and legs as his body worked to fight the sand. A pool of perspiration had already settled in the little clump of dark hair that rested at the base of Ben's spine, just above the swell of his perfect ass. Paulie longed to lay his tongue there and lap the perspiration away. Then he forced himself to stop thinking those thoughts. He should be happy just having Ben here as a friend. After all, only a few weeks ago he had been convinced he would never see Ben again. The last thing he wanted to do was risk this second chance for renewing their friendship by crossing the line again. Doing the wrong thing. Letting his urges override his common sense.

Ben pointed to a cormorant perched on a rock at the edge of the beach, where a small landslide had carried the cliff down to the sand. The cormorant was pecking at a fish he held in his webbed feet, ignoring the two humans, centered on his own quest for life. He perched there, loftily fearless, as if the beach belonged solely to him and he damn well knew it.

Up ahead, they saw the long pier that stretched out into the Pacific from Scripps Institute of Oceanography. They passed it and ventured farther up the coast, not yet feeling the need to turn around and head back. They had only come a couple of miles, even if the sand pull did make it feel like ten.

As they ran, the beach became more crowded. They were away from the residential areas now, and the coastline was more rugged, with steep cliffs reaching high to their right and the surf pounding even more determinedly at the shore than it had a couple of miles back. There were more surfers here, most in wetsuits. The water was cold. Their cars were parked in the dirt and scrub up alongside the coastal highway at the top of the cliff. Ben and Paulie watched several of the surfers carefully navigating down the rocky cliffs to get to the water, lugging their surfboards along with them, dragging coolers and towels and even the occasional kid down the dangerous inclines. Eager for the thrill of catching a few waves, they were willing to risk life and limb to get to a place where they could do it. In their own way, they were as fearless and proprietary as the cormorant two miles back. They seemed to regard the beach as their own personal property. And Paulie was glad to see it because he happened to agree with them wholeheartedly. The coastline *did* belong to everyone.

"Black's Beach coming up," Ben panted at his side.

And sure enough, up ahead was the first glimpse of naked bodies they had seen. This clothing optional section of the California coast was world famous, and the locals and tourists made thorough use of it. Sometimes more than nude sunbathing went on in the sand beneath the hot California sun, but even that was simply part of the experience.

Ben and Paulie kept their eyes straight ahead for the most part as they jogged through the sea of nude sunbathers. Soon the naked people thinned out, and the beach narrowed to a tiny strip of sand heralding the end of Black's Beach and the beginning of an area only wide enough for runners and hikers to navigate.

Hemmed in by the ocean on one side and the jumbled boulders of a dozen landslides on the other, Ben stumbled to a stop, and Paulie stopped along with him. Looking ahead and behind, they found themselves alone.

Ben pointed to the rocks. "Let's sit for a few minutes."

Paulie's heart was thudding from the exertion, just as Ben's was. He wiped the sweat from his eyes with the bandanna, then tied it back around his neck.

"All right," Paulie said, dragging his fingers through his sweaty hair to get it back off his face.

Ben took him by the arm and led him to a shelf of rock as big as a semi that had at some point or other, either last week or a thousand years ago, slid down the cliff to land by the water.

They sat on the stone's edge, pulled off their shoes and socks, and let the gentle surf periodically wash across their feet. The cool water felt good.

They stared out at the sea, then gradually turned to face each other.

The beauty and sheer happiness in Ben's smile almost made Paulie's heart stop cold. For the first time since his arrival, Ben looked totally content.

Ben was clearly thrilled to be home. And Paulie was thrilled for him.

Chapter 8

"YOU LOOK happy," Paulie said.

Ben dug his thumbs into the quads in his left leg, massaging the muscles like maybe they were bothering him. But he smiled while he did it. He extended his leg a couple of times, flexing, unflexing. He gazed out across the water, then closed his eyes and tilted his head back, letting the wind dry the sweat off his face. "Does it show?"

"Yeah," Paulie said, now smiling too. "It does." He studied Ben's face. With his eyes closed, the man looked—*less*. Less than he was when his eyes were open. Less than when he was soaking up the world around him through those gorgeous brown orbs. Still handsome. Still stunning. Just—*less.*

Paulie's own legs were fine. He ran in the sand almost every day. Still, it took a bit of getting used to. Paulie knew that. Ben knew it too. Paulie wondered if Ben would get a cramp in his sleep tonight from the sand running they had done during the day.

He looked down at Ben's feet. Sure enough, Ben's big toenail was missing from the left foot.

"You really did lose a toenail," Paulie said.

Ben smiled, his eyes still closed. The sea breeze whipped the hair around his face. "Told you." And after a pause, he added, "It's good being with you again, Paulie. I've really missed you."

Paulie was able to study Ben's face because Ben's eyes were still shut, his head still tilted back as he savored the feel of the sun and the wind. It was almost as if he kept his eyes closed purposely, as if giving Paulie a *chance* to study him.

And suddenly Paulie knew the time was right to say some things that needed to be said. In fact, there might never be a better opportunity. "I've missed you too, Ben. I hated the way it—it all ended."

Ben turned and faced Paulie then, pushing the hair from his eyes, squinting against the sudden light. "Did you?" he asked.

Paulie had to look away. He tried to cover it by examining his own missing toenail. "Yep. I've been wanting to say this for a long time, Ben. I'm sorry I crossed the line." He finally looked up and their eyes met. "I'm sorry I did what I did that night, Ben. I was drunk but it was still no excuse."

Ben shrugged. "I was drunk too."

"I know," Paulie said. "That was *another* reason I shouldn't have done what I did. You were—susceptible. Wait, that's not the right word. You were—"

Ben's smile had never left his face. "I was an easy target."

Paulie didn't like the sound of that, but he couldn't very well disagree since it was basically the truth. "Yes," he said. "You were an easy target. You couldn't defend yourself."

At that, Ben laughed a throaty laugh. He seemed to find that really funny. "Oh, I think I could have defended myself if I wanted to."

Paulie could feel the blood infusing his face. He hated it when he blushed. "Well, I just want you to know that I've learned my lesson. I'll be good from now on. I promise. I almost lost your friendship once over my own stupidity, and once was enough. You don't have to be afraid it will happen again."

"I'm not afraid, Paulie."

The wind was picking up. It was Paulie's turn to push the hair out of his eyes. "You're not?"

"No." Ben gave Paulie an easy smile, then turned to face the ocean again. He watched a tern fly overhead before he spoke. "I've thought about it a lot, what happened that night."

"Oh God," Paulie groaned, growing more embarrassed by the minute.

Ben elbowed him to shut him up. "No. What I mean to say is, I've thought about *you* a lot since that night."

"Yeah, you thought about whether you ever wanted to see me again."

Ben's smile fell away. "You don't really believe that, do you?"

"Well, yeah. It's been forever since you came around. What else was I supposed to believe?"

"I was working, Paulie. I was working halfway across the country. I *couldn't* very well come around."

Paulie wasn't buying it. "There were summers."

"I had summer school classes then. Makeup work for the slower students. That would have been the *worst* time to leave Omaha."

Paulie still wasn't buying it. "You could have phoned or e-mailed or written me a fucking letter."

And with that, Paulie knew, he had finally struck a nerve.

Ben looked away. "I know. I could have done that."

"So why didn't you?" Paulie asked. "It would have saved me a lot of heartache. I thought I'd lost your friendship forever, Ben. All because of one stupid drunken act of—"

"It's not because I hated you that I didn't come around, Paulie. It's not because of what you did that night. What *we* did. Please tell me you don't really believe that."

"Then what was it? The next morning you were gone. You didn't get within fifty feet of me at the graduation ceremony. What was I supposed to think, Ben?"

Ben shifted around on the stone ledge to better face Paulie, so Paulie immediately did the same. They sat there at the edge of the continent, cross-legged, facing each other as their hair thrashed in the wind and the salt spray cooled their sun-heated skin.

When Ben reached out to take Paulie's hand, Paulie was stunned for a moment. Then he accepted it the way it was meant. In friendship. Nothing more. He let his hand be cradled in Ben's warm grasp. And even now, after all his bullshit about being sorry, Paulie felt urges rise up he had just sworn he would never set loose again.

Ben gazed down at Paulie's hand for a second before speaking. When he did finally speak, Ben raised his head and centered his eyes on Paulie's face.

"I need to tell you some things," Ben said.

Paulie wasn't sure he liked the sound of that. "All right."

Ben had the look of a man who has thought long and hard about what he wants to say. Paulie suddenly knew without a doubt that whatever Ben was about to tell him, he had already made up his mind to tell it before he ever drove those fifteen hundred miles back to San Diego. Good or bad, this was important to Ben, and Paulie cared for the man enough to give him his full attention.

Because that's what friends do.

Now that he was down to the wire, Ben suddenly seemed to lose his resolve. He tore his eyes from Paulie's face for a moment and stared out at the water. Then he gazed down at their clenched hands again. And finally, he focused his attention once more on Paulie's face. When he did, Paulie could see the determination there. The determination to say what he had come here to say.

Whatever the hell that was.

"Remember our last year of college?" Ben asked.

Paulie had to grin. "That's a rhetorical question, right? Hell yes, I remember it."

Ben nodded. "You remember it from your end, Paulie. Now I'm going to tell you how I remember it from my end."

Paulie gave his head a tiny shake. "I don't understand."

"I know," Ben said. "I know you don't."

Paulie smiled, thinking he could make Ben relax a bit. He seemed tense. "Then elucidate me."

The smile that was meant to relax Ben didn't work at all. Again Ben gazed out at the water. He looked pensive, Paulie thought. Then Paulie thought, no. He looks—uncomfortable. As if whatever Ben was about to tell him was something he really didn't want to say but felt he should.

Paulie exerted pressure on Ben's hand, just a little squeeze, to get his attention. "What is it? Tell me."

Ben took a tiny shuddering breath, and after a final glance at Paulie's hand in his, he brought his eyes up until the two men were once again gazing at each other. "I learned some things while I was in Omaha, Paulie. I told you last night I learned I need my friends around me. But I learned something more than that."

"Did you?"

"Yeah." A self-deprecating little smile turned up the corners of Ben's mouth. He licked the salt spray from his lips. "I learned some things about myself."

"Like what? And what does that have to do with our final year at college?"

Ben released Paulie's hand. The wind was getting stronger. He pushed his hair out of his eyes. "It has everything to do with it. That last year was the longest year of my life."

Paulie was surprised to feel hurt by that remark. "I thought it was a great year," he said, sounding defensive even to his own ears. "I thought we were having fun."

"We were." Ben smiled. "It was living with you that drove me crazy."

Paulie's face fell. He could even feel it falling. It was like the Great Puppeteer had just cut his strings. "Why? I thought—"

"Paulie, I'm not talking about you. I'm talking about me. Me being *around* you. It was a strange time for me. I'm not used to having to hide my feelings day in and day out."

Paulie was beginning to get a little pissed off. "Goddamn it, Ben. Spit it out. What feelings were you trying to hide? And why are you beating around the bush like this? If you have something to say, just say it. Are you sorry we were roommates? Is that it? If it is, it's a little late to—"

Paulie was shocked to see Ben laugh. "Don't be stupid, Paulie. You were a great roommate."

"Then what was it?" Paulie snapped.

And as if Paulie wasn't being annoyed enough, Ben reached out and tousled Paulie's hair again, like maybe the wind wasn't doing a good enough job of it and Ben thought he could help it along.

"Calm down, Tiger. I'm trying to explain to you about that night. That last night."

"Yes," Paulie hissed, tired of talking about that night. Tired of hearing about it. "The night I fucked up. What about it?"

"That year was really confusing for me, Paulie." Ben giggled. "Sort of like this conversation right now is confusing for you."

Paulie narrowed his eyes; then he thought he probably looked too mean doing that, so he spat up an insincere chuckle to soften the look. "Confused is right, dipshit. I don't know what the hell you're talking about."

"It was confusing because I didn't really understand my feelings." Ben gave a satisfied sigh, as if finally finding relief in having said the words he had long wanted to say. He looked expectantly at Paulie's face.

But the words and the look meant nothing to Paulie. He still didn't know what the hell the man was getting at. "Christ, Ben, could you please just come out with it and tell me what you're trying to say before I pick you up off this rock and throw you in the fucking ocean."

At that, a mischievous light entered Ben's eyes. "You could *try*," he said.

If it was a wrestling match Ben wanted, Paulie didn't take the bait. Instead, Paulie forced himself to calm down. "What feelings are you talking about? Tell me that much. And what did they have to do with that night? And why was it the longest fucking year of your life? Shit, Ben. Answer at least *one* of those questions."

"Okay. And the answers are all tied in together, so it won't take long."

Paulie rolled his eyes at the heavens. "It's *already* taken long."

"Impatient prick," Ben muttered, flashing a dimple.

"You betcha."

Ben scratched the back of his neck. Then he flicked a bug off his forearm. After that he tucked one leg under the other, immediately decided that wasn't comfortable, and dropped it back over the edge of the rock. Killing time. Even Paulie could see that was what he was doing.

Finally, he looked Paulie full in the face and said, "What happened that night was something I had wanted to happen for months. I wanted to feel your mouth on me, Paulie. I wanted you to suck my cock the way you did. I wanted you to taste my come. Everything that happened that night was something I had been dreaming about for months."

Paulie was stunned. "Jesus, Ben. If you wanted a blowjob, all you had to do was ask."

Ben nodded. "I know. But I couldn't. I just couldn't. I knew if anything like that happened, it would only happen if you made the first move. The night we got drunk, you finally did."

Paulie couldn't believe it. "And you wanted this to happen all year?"

Ben nodded. His face was red. Really red, but he was obviously determined to finish what he had started. "Yes," he said. "Every single day I wanted it to happen."

Paulie's brain was suddenly lashed by whips of memory. One right after the other. Ben standing naked at the kitchen counter, pouring a cup of coffee. Ben toweling his naked body as he strode through the apartment, not caring that Paulie could see him. Ben nude, slinging his leg over the kitchen chair, genitals swinging, and plopping himself down across from Paulie, who was sitting there pretending to study.

Paulie began to understand at last. "You really did want it to happen. That's why you paraded around naked half the time."

Ben blushed even redder. "Yes."

Paulie examined Ben's face, Ben's eyes, still trying to get a handle on what he had just been told. "But then, when it finally did happen, why did you disappear like you did? You left in the middle of the night. I thought you were disgusted by what I'd done. I thought our friendship was over. Hell, even *I* thought it was inexcusable what I did. And you simply left and let me think it."

Again, Ben took Paulie's hand. "I know. I'm sorry. And I did leave because I was disgusted. But I was disgusted with myself, not you. I was embarrassed."

"But why? It was just a blowjob, Ben. I didn't do any permanent damage to your precious—"

Ben interrupted. "Don't get mad, Paulie. Please. I was confused back then. We were young. People get confused about stuff when they're young."

Paulie's words were clipped. Terse. "It was only two years ago, Ben. We weren't *that* fucking young."

Paulie tried to calm down. He decided to take the high ground and attempt to lower his own sense of betrayal. And then he thought, no, maybe I won't. Because I do feel betrayed. Betrayed that I should be left to feel guilty all this time for something Ben wanted to happen all along.

"So how was it?" he coolly asked. "Was it worth the wait? Was it everything you hoped it would be?"

Ben looked as if he had been slapped. "I never meant to hurt you, Paulie. I was just trying to straighten out my own head. To understand the feelings I was feeling."

"Well, Christ, Ben, they're pretty straightforward feelings, don't you think? I don't see anything much confusing about them. You wanted me to suck your dick, and I finally did. That's all that happened. Of course, then you left me to simmer in my own guilt for two fucking years thinking I had lost the best friend I ever had *because* I sucked his dick. How could you do that, Ben? The blowjob was nothing. But that last part is a heartbreaker."

"Paulie, I—"

"And by the way, Ben. That was a pretty long year for me too, you know. Wanting you every minute. Jacking off in my room to the sound of you snoring through the wall. Watching you parade around naked and wanting to reach out every time you did and pull you to me and just *feel* you. Just *feel* your skin. *Feel* your warmth. God, I had a crush on you that whole year. I was so fucking nuts about you it's a wonder I graduated at all. Hell, it wouldn't be much of an exaggeration to say I was in love with you, Ben. Bet you didn't know that, did you? Huh?"

Ben's eyes were sad. He watched Paulie through the saddest eyes Paulie had ever seen. But somehow those sad eyes didn't quite touch Paulie's heart. He wasn't in the mood for it.

"Yes, Paulie. I did know. But you were a gentleman right up to the end. It really drove me nuts how much of a gentleman you were. In the end it took a couple of kegs of beer to knock it out of you."

"Funny," Paulie said. "Very funny."

"Paulie, please don't be mad. I'm only telling you this because I want you to know why I left you hanging all this time. I'm not trying to hurt you all over again. I was ashamed of myself for doing what I did. And I was ashamed of myself for—"

"Ashamed of yourself for what?"

Tears sparkled Ben's eyes. "Ashamed of myself for enjoying it so much."

Paulie simply stared. Somewhere high above his head a seabird screamed.

"You know, Ben. That shame you're talking about is how I live my life. That's the kind of sex I have with people. It's who I am and what I do. It's what all your friends back at the house do. It's how we all live our lives. I'm sorry if you think it's a shameful way to live. And I'm sorry I dragged you down to our shame-infested shithole of an existence. But if it's any consolation, now you've made me see the shame in it too. So now I guess maybe we're in the same boat."

Ben clutched his arm. The light had gone out of his eyes. "Paulie, that's not what I meant."

Paulie gently pulled his arm free and started pulling on his socks. "We should be getting back. I've got company to entertain."

"Paulie, please—"

"It'll be time for dinner soon. The caterers will be arriving with chow." He handed Ben his shoes, averting his eyes. "You up to running back, or should I go on ahead and let you walk to give your legs a break? I know you're not used to the sand."

Ben's voice was flat. Emotionless. "Sure, Paulie. You go ahead. I'll just amble back at my own pace." He looked at the shoes and socks in his hands as if he couldn't quite remember who they belonged to. "I won't be long."

"Later, then," Paulie said, and without a backward glance, he headed off down the beach at a dead run, kicking up sand in his wake. Getting away. Just getting away.

He could feel his face burning with embarrassment. No, not embarrassment, he told himself. Shame. Ben was right. That's exactly what it was. Pure, unadulterated shame.

And when that realization entered his head, he ran all the faster. Running from the shame. Running from Ben.

Never looking back.

DINNER WAS an awkward affair, at least in Paulie's mind. Every time he and Ben came within ten feet of each other, he felt himself drawing back, turning away. There was something about the words Ben had spoken on the beach that made Paulie remember that Indiana Jones movie where the bad guy reached in and pulled out people's hearts. Just pulled them right out of their fucking chests.

If the other guests noticed anything amiss between Paulie and Ben, they were too wrapped up in their own little dramas to worry about it. Jack was still hanging all over Jeffrey, which Jeffrey didn't seem to be minding at all. Trevor and Jamie, with Danny still parked in the middle, were still hanging all over each other as well. It was all a booze-fueled fuck fest is what it was. The way everyone was acting, Paulie figured his stockpile of alcoholic beverages must by now be seriously depleted. He'd have to make a booze run in the morning.

Funny. He'd thought there would be tantrums and histrionics from the way the original love affairs had self-destructed then shifted around since everyone's arrival, which was little more than twenty-four hours ago. Could you believe *that?* But so far the only two people who seemed upset by the way things were panning out were Paulie and Ben, and they were the only two who weren't lovers to begin with. And even between Paulie and Ben, Paulie was the only one who appeared angry. Ben seemed simply hurt.

Paulie was already feeling guilty about what had happened out there on the beach. He knew he had overreacted. Now here he was perhaps on the verge of losing Ben as a friend not much more than five minutes after getting him *back* as a friend. Jesus, maybe their friendship simply wasn't meant to be. Or maybe Paulie's feelings for Ben were too strong to let himself be limited to friendship. It's hard enough being nuts about somebody when they are not around, but when they are near, it's even harder. Seeing them every minute. Wondering what they're thinking. Longing to reach out. Longing to touch.

In the middle of his salad, before Paulie ever got to the main course at dinner, which happened to be Italian cuisine, (the caterers had apparently ignored Paulie's suggestion of cutting back on the calories), he started pouring his own drinks because Jeffrey was too light on the touch. Paulie wanted a drink that would kick some sense into him. Or knock him out completely. He didn't much care which it turned out to be as long as it took his mind off Ben.

And speaking of Ben, the man was playing with his food, not even pretending to eat. He was watching Paulie's every move. Watching him pour those heavy-handed drinks. Knowing Paulie was doing it because he was upset. Upset with the things Ben had said. Upset with the way Paulie had *taken* the things Ben had said.

In the midst of a ribald and raunchy joke Trevor was telling about an imam with a two-headed dildo and a Shiite prostitute with one leg and an overbite, Ben suddenly pushed himself from the table, said something about having a headache, and stalked off to his room. Everyone at the table watched him walk away, and the minute he was gone, they turned to Paulie.

If Paulie noticed them staring at him, he didn't let on. "Cheers," Paulie said, raising his glass to the empty doorway Ben had just walked through.

While Paulie was obviously getting drunk, his tone somehow managed to sober the rest of the group up. And wasn't that a bummer.

"What the hell happened out there on that beach today?" Trevor asked, leaning over his lasagna and tapping Paulie on the arm with a breadstick.

"Nothing," Paulie lied. "We just ran."

They were having dinner in the formal dining room. Jeffrey circled the table in his pristinely white houseboy uniform, pouring wine into wine glasses, clearing away little messes and dirty plates, doing his job but ogling Jack while he did it. Jack sat by himself at the end of the long rectangular table opposite Paulie. Jamie, Trevor, and Danny were crunched in together on one side of the table because they couldn't bear to be apart, while the other side was empty. It looked like the last fucking supper, for Christ's sake, with everybody hogging one side of the table. Candles were lit, the chandelier was glowing warmly overhead, a bit of soft chamber music was playing in the background. And the whole damn dinner arrangement looked cattywampus with everyone sitting at one side of the table like that.

Paulie held up his glass while the houseboy topped off his wine. When Jeffrey was finished, Paulie said, "Take off that stupid white waiter's jacket and have dinner with us, Jeffrey. And Jack, drag your chair around to the side here so you and Jeff can sit together."

He didn't have to ask twice. Jeffrey set a place for himself opposite Trevor. Jack squeaked his chair along the hardwood floor and dragged his plates and silverware along afterward. When the table was arranged the way they wanted it, Jeffrey dragged all the caterer's pots and pans filled with their dinner items from the kitchen and placed them along the center of the table. When he was finished, he announced, "Let's do it home style, gentlemen. From now on, everybody serve themselves."

Paulie smiled when Jeffrey tugged off his server's jacket and tossed it across the room. He sat down beside Jack in his white T-shirt and slacks, and Jack snuggled up to him with a radiant smile on his face. They each had one arm visible above the table. Paulie suspected they were holding hands with the other two. And wasn't that just romantic as hell?

He turned to Jamie. "Looks like you and Jack are no longer an item." There didn't seem to be much point in holding his voice down about it since the two in question, Jack and Jeffrey, were sitting there in front of God and everybody practically climbing all over each other anyway.

Jamie gave a cavalier shrug. "Ah, well. Everybody's got to do what everybody's got to do." He turned to Danny who was sitting between him and Trevor. "Right, lover?"

"Right," Danny said, bringing both hands up and cupping Jamie's face with one and Trevor's face with the other. The two men leaned in and gave Danny a peck on either side of his neck. Then they each waggled a tongue in Danny's ears. Danny giggled and squirmed around in his chair.

When they were finished and Danny had calmed down a bit, Trevor rolled his eyes back to Paulie. "Seems to me the only one being left out is the hostess. You need a date, Paulie. And preferably one that isn't straight. You never did have enough sense to fall in love with the right man, did you?"

Paulie smiled a noncommittal smile and downed the dregs of his wine. Then he poured himself another glassful while the grandfather clock in the hallway chimed the hour. Ten o'clock.

Tossing down his napkin and snatching up his wine glass and a couple of breadsticks, Paulie announced, "On that note, I think I'll hit the hay. You guys enjoy the rest of your dinner. Try not to smash the Spode."

"What the fuck is a Spode?" Jeffrey asked.

Paulie laughed. "The china."

"Oh."

Paulie gathered up what little dignity he had left and said his good-nights. Already blinking back the beginnings of a wine headache, he tottered off toward the stairs.

As he reeled up the steps, he grandly announced to no one in particular, "I'm going the fuck to bed. Don't like it? Bite me."

Halfway up, he felt a tap on his shoulder. He turned to find Jeffrey there.

"You all right, massa?"

"Knock off the slave talk, Jeff. It's annoying as hell."

Jeffrey blinked. "Sorry."

Paulie could feel his eyes beginning to close of their own volition. "Did you need something?"

"Yes, sir. I was wondering if you would mind if I moved to the front of the bus."

Paulie smiled. "Rooming with Jack, huh?"

"Yeah. He says he has an opening."

"I'll bet he does."

Jeffrey looked a little uncomfortable, but determined. Paulie smiled inside to see how much the man wanted this to happen.

Jeffrey cleared his throat and tried again. "Jack and I were figuring since Jamie has moved in with the two white gentlemen, sorry, with Trevor and Danny, then we couldn't see much reason for us to be sleeping apart when Jack has that whole bigass bed all to himself."

"Makes sense to me," Paulie said.

Jeffrey grinned. His white teeth flashed. "Does that mean yes?"

"Yes. That means yes."

"Thanks, boss. I mean, Paulie. I mean, sir."

"Paulie's fine."

"Paulie."

"If there's nothing else, Jeffrey, I'll be toddling off to bed now before I fall flat on my face."

"Have a good night."

"You too," Paulie turned away.

He smiled to hear a little tap dancing going on behind him on the marble steps.

"Nighty night, Bojangles," Paulie muttered and chuckled off up the stairs.

Chapter 9

IT WAS midnight when Paulie heard the knock on his bedroom door. He listened, not sure if the knock had been in his drunken dream or in real life. When it came again he knew it was real. That was when he checked the clock to see what time it was.

Aside from the knocking, the house was silent. Everyone must have gone to bed. He looked under a tangle of sheets at the foot of his bed and saw Hammer peeking out, wondering why he was being disturbed at this ungodly hour. Paulie gave him a tender pat on the head and told him to go back to sleep. Being a good dog, and lazy as hell, two seconds later he did.

Paulie was naked. He pulled a robe around himself while rubbing the sleep boogers out of his eyes. As he was doing that, he half-heartedly tried to prod his hair into a semblance of something other than a fucking tumbleweed. He opened his door, expecting to find Jack, crying about losing Jamie. Or Trevor, crying about sharing Danny. Or Danny, crying about being worn out from trying to pleasure two men at once. Or Jeffrey, crying about Jack's ass being so loose it was like sticking his dick in the trunk of a car.

What Paulie *didn't* expect was to find no one there. The hallway was empty.

Then he heard the knock again, this time *behind* him, and he realized it was coming from the connecting door to the other bedroom.

Ben's bedroom.

What he had been hoping would happen, now was indeed about to happen. Ben was truly going to come walking through that connecting door. And now that he was, Paulie wasn't ready at all. He wasn't even sure if he was still mad or hurt or confused or what. Wasn't that just the way these things happened? You get your head around a dream, and then the dream flies off in the wrong direction every time.

More than likely Ben was simply coming to tell him he would be leaving in the morning.

That thought made an ache settle in Paulie's heart. It was so strong, he almost clutched his chest. Instead, he forced a resigned expression to his face and moved toward the door.

Not letting himself think too much about it, he simply yanked the door open and stepped back, expecting the worst.

Ben was wearing a tumbleweed on his head too. And like Paulie, he was also wearing a robe. If one of the men hadn't been light haired and the other dark, they would have looked like sloppy-ass twins. They even had the same nervous, disheveled expression on their faces.

"Can I come in?" Ben asked, his voice a little hoarse. He sounded like someone who has just woken up.

Ben was so gorgeous standing there with his messed-up hair and his fuzzy legs poking out the bottom of the robe that it took Paulie a moment to find his voice.

Ben took his hesitation for reluctance. "If you'd rather I didn't...."

Paulie snapped out of it. "No, Ben. Come on in. Don't mind me. I think I killed a few brain cells what with all the booze I drank at dinner."

Ben stepped into the room and turned to stand in front of Paulie. "That was my fault for pissing you off out on the beach. I'm sorry."

Paulie pointed to a couple of high-backed leather chairs parked in front of the unlit fireplace. "Sit. And it wasn't your fault. It was mine. I was embarrassed, so I did what I always do when I get embarrassed. I threw it back in someone else's face. This time it happened to be you."

Ben sat in one chair while Paulie perched on the arm of the one across from him. Both men tucked their robes between their legs almost primly, considering their past. Ben was the only one who seemed to take note of that fact. A tiny smile tipped the corner of his mouth before he studiously wiped it away.

"Paulie, you were embarrassed because I said everything wrong out there on that stupid rock. I was still tired from the long drive. I hadn't run on sand for a while. I was pooped." Ben clapped his mouth shut, then said, "Oh, who the hell am I kidding. I said everything wrong out there because I was embarrassed too. I'm sorry if I hurt your feelings, Paulie. I honestly didn't mean to."

Paulie relaxed a little. He slid down to sit on the chair like a proper adult. He again tucked the robe between his legs. For lack of anything better to do with his nervous hands, he fiddled with the belt of his robe. "It's okay. I—"

"No, Paulie, it's not okay. I don't feel shame about what we did that night. I've never felt shame about it. And for you to think that I equate shame with the way you and Jamie and Trevor live your lives really broke my heart. It couldn't be further from the truth. I—I love all you guys. I would never think that."

Paulie smiled. "I know you well enough to know you're not a homophobic asshole. I guess you just hit a nerve this afternoon. I'm sorry for getting all pissy and diva-esque about it. I can be a real prick sometimes."

It was Ben's turn to smile. "I think I'll let that one stand."

They were both grinning now. "I thought you might," Paulie said.

Ben gazed around the room, still embarrassed by all that had taken place on the beach, but obviously determined to get past it. "You've changed things since your grandmother had this room. She had flowers everywhere, I remember. And knickknacks. Millions of knickknacks."

Paulie laughed. "Yeah. Our cleaning lady was glad to see those go."

"I'll bet."

"You left the dinner table early," Paulie said. "You hungry? You want to raid the fridge?"

Ben patted his stomach. "Naw. I'm good. Unless you want to."

"Naw. I'm good too," Paulie said.

They settled into a comfortable silence. Paulie was so relieved to be speaking to Ben again, he didn't even mind the vicious little headache still niggling around inside his noggin from all the booze he drank at dinner.

Finally, Ben appeared to remember why he'd knocked on Paulie's door in the middle of the night.

"Paulie, there was something else I didn't tell you on the beach today. Well, several things actually. I was just getting warmed up out there when you stormed off in a prissy huff, if you don't mind my characterizing it as such. It's not homophobic to call someone a prissy huffmeister, is it?" Ben was grinning.

"Not if the pump fits." Paulie grinned back. Then, only half joking, Paulie buried his face in his hands. "Oh Lord, you aren't going to piss me off again, are you? If you are I may need to make a booze run before you start talking. Prissy huffs create such a thirst, and my other houseguests have pretty well obliterated my stockpile of alcoholic beverages, the drunken louts."

Ben smiled for a moment before his face sobered. He leaned forward in the chair, decided he still wasn't close enough to Paulie, and proceeded to hop the chair a foot or so in Paulie's direction. After that, when he leaned forward, he was able to rest his hand on Paulie's knee.

Paulie's *bare* knee.

Paulie eyed Ben's hand like he had never seen one quite like it before. It felt warm and comforting against his skin. When Ben moved his thumb in a wee stroking movement across the hair on Paulie's leg, Paulie felt a sudden rush of desire such as he hadn't felt for a very long time.

Ben gazed down at his own hand, then up to Paulie's face.

"That last year when we were sharing the apartment truly was a long year, Paulie."

"You told me that."

Ben nodded. "I know. But you didn't let me carry the thought to its ultimate destination. If you'll shut the fuck up for a minute, I'd like to try to do that now."

Paulie locked his lips shut with an imaginary key and tossed the key in the fireplace.

Ben's dimples flashed. First one, then the other. "Thank you." He inhaled a deep breath and tried again. "I was confused about my feelings. Hell, I was confused about everything that year. Like you, it's a wonder I graduated at all."

"What were you confused about, aside from wishing I'd suck your dick?"

Ben's eyes narrowed. "You promised to shut up."

"Oops, sorry. Go ahead."

Ben dragged his fingers through his hair. His other hand still rested on Paulie's knee. And now he gave that knee a gentle squeeze. "Not only was I confused by my feelings, but I was confused by something else. It wasn't just the whole sex scenario thing I was fantasizing about. You know, the dick thing. But it was something else."

Paulie threw his hands in the air like a man waiting for a basketball to come sailing toward him. "Jesus Christ, Ben, would you get to the fucking point!"

Ben gave his forehead a frantic rub, as if thinking maybe he could get the thoughts moving around in his head that way, stir them up, make the good ones settle on top. "Well…. It's sort of like… uh… well…."

"Jesus! Spit it out!"

Ben released Paulie's knee and collapsed back in his chair. Now it was Ben's turn to put his hands over his face. "I had a crush on you too, Paulie. I did. Just like you had a crush on me, I had a crush on you. There. I fucking said it." He peeked out between his fingers to see how Paulie was reacting.

Paulie was reacting by staring at him. That's all. Simply staring.

Ben seemed thankful Paulie wasn't talking, although he might have been a little disconcerted by the look of total amazement that had wiped all other emotion from Paulie's face. Every smidgeon of it. He looked like a man who'd just had a brain fart, and it damn near killed him.

"Don't have a stroke quite yet, Paulie. There's more."

"Oh, good," Paulie managed to say.

Again, Ben leaned forward. This time he placed his hands at the side of Paulie's knees. Both hands, both knees. Sort of cradling Paulie's legs between his big, beautiful paws. "I learned who I was in Omaha, Paulie."

"That's nice," Paulie said. "And who did you turn out to be?"

Ben sighed. "Don't freak."

"I never freak."

Ben sighed again. "I'm gay. Just like you. Just like Jamie and Trevor. I guess I just couldn't face it until I got away from you—and them—and my parents—and made peace with it on my own."

Now it was Paulie's turn to lean forward. He still looked stunned, and he knew it. But even knowing it couldn't knock the stun off his face. "You mean you came out while you were gone? You actually—came out? You're a gay man?"

"Yes."

"You actually came the fuck out?"

"Yes."

"In *Nebraska? Nobody* comes out in Nebraska."

Ben laughed. "Not true, Paulie. I did. But you're missing the big picture here."

Ben's hands were still cradling Paulie's knees. Paulie laid his own hands over them. "My God, Ben. What could be a bigger picture than the fact that you're gay?"

This time Ben blushed as he spoke. "Because I didn't tell you the truth on the beach about something else. I lied to you. Flat out lied. I froze up and I lied."

"Okay, you lied. About what?" Paulie asked, still trying to get his head around the fact that Ben was gay. The man was actually fucking gay.

"About the fact that I was homesick for San Diego."

"You mean you weren't?"

"Well, yeah, I was. But I wasn't just homesick."

"Why?" Paulie asked. "What else was it?"

Ben pulled his hands away and buried them in his hair. He held his hair back off his face as he stared up at the ceiling as if incapable of saying what he was about to say while looking at Paulie's face.

"I wasn't just homesick, Paulie. I was—"

"You were what? Spit it out," Paulie begged. He was getting tired of hanging onto Ben's every word like a cat hanging on a curtain. His fingernails were starting to hurt.

"I can't," Ben said. "I can't say it."

"You *can't say it?* What the hell do you mean you can't say it?"

Ben swallowed. Paulie could hear the little gulping sound he made when he did it.

When Ben stood, Paulie's jaw dropped. "Where do you think you're going?"

"I need to be alone for a minute."

"You need to be alone for a minute! You tell me my best straight friend who I've had a misdirected crush on since freshman year in college is actually gay and now you need to be alone?"

"Yes. I need to be alone."

"To do what?"

"To brush my teeth."

"You need to brush your *teeth*?"

"Yes."

"Look, asswipe. This isn't the time for oral hygiene."

"Yes it is. I need to brush my teeth and go back to bed."

"You want to go back to *bed*?"

Ben stared down at Paulie still sitting in the big leather chair looking up at him. Paulie was looking at him like he was crazy, and who could blame the man for that? Ben made a tiny motion with his hand as if he meant to reach out and touch Paulie, but at the last moment he pulled back. Then he turned and walked from the room, quietly closing the connecting door behind him.

Paulie gave the door his best laser beam gaze to deconstruct the fucking thing and burn it out of the way, but it didn't work. A moment later he heard water running in the other bathroom. *Ben really is brushing his teeth. Is he nuts?*

Paulie hurled himself out of the chair and strode toward the door. With his hand two inches from the knob, he stopped. He could still hear water running, and now there was a scrubbing sound accompanying it. The fucker was actually brushing his teeth!

And for lack of a better plan, and because his mouth tasted like the bottom of a chicken coop, Paulie spun on his heel, madder than hell, and stormed into his own bathroom. He squirted enough toothpaste onto his toothbrush to wash a car and stuck it in his mouth. He brushed and brushed and brushed until the froth was dribbling off his chin and down his arm, splashing the sink, spattering the mirror—making a hell of a mess, but who the hell cared?

How could he just spill his guts, then walk away like that? And gay! Ben is gay!

Paulie stopped brushing and stared at himself in the mirror while the toothpaste foam dribbled down the front of his robe.

Now what? Every fantasy he had ever entertained concerning a nakedass Ben would now be bombarding Paulie every two minutes, and he would no longer have the luxury of knowing it was all a pipe dream. Was he now being given the opportunity to act on his fantasies, knowing Ben was gay? Did he dare to hope the man might even respond favorably? Or would the fact that Ben was gay now make the whole fantasy thing even more uncomfortable for both of them? The fact that Ben was gay didn't change the fact they were still, first and foremost, friends. Did it? And who said Ben wanted any more than that? Ben certainly hadn't.

Paulie was about to choke on the toothpaste froth, so he spat it out, rinsed his mouth with water, gargled for what seemed an hour and a half because he wasn't sure what he was going to do when he *finished* gargling, and that's when he heard the noise behind him.

He wiped the toothpaste crap off the mirror with his hand, which actually smeared it even worse, and saw Ben standing at the bathroom door watching him.

Ben seemed to suddenly have found the courage to speak.

"Coming out was hard for me, Paulie. I don't know why, it just was. The truth was hard for me to accept. But remembering that one drunken night we shared made me see the truth better than anything else ever had. I—I've never experienced anything like that, Paulie. The way your skin felt beneath my hands. The way you trembled in my arms. The way you wanted me. I'm sorry I left the way I did, leaving you feeling guilty about what happened. Especially since it really wasn't your fault. It was mine. Absolutely mine."

Paulie wiped a towel over his mouth. "Ben—"

"Let me talk," Ben pleaded. "Let me finish."

And Paulie nodded, standing mute with the towel still pressed to his mouth. Waiting.

Ben brushed the hair off his forehead. His eyes never left Paulie's face.

"And now here we are together again, and you're walking on eggshells because you think you did something wrong and you think I hate you for it, and I'm walking on eggshells just hoping you'll notice me again. Like you did that last year in the apartment. I liked having you want me like that, Paulie. I liked seeing the hunger in your eyes when I walked past. And if only you had looked closer, you might have seen the hunger in *my* eyes."

"I never knew," Paulie breathed. "I never *imagined.*"

"I know," Ben said. "I know you didn't. And after that night— after we did what we did—I had no choice but to leave. The job in Nebraska was already a done deal. I had to go. And in a way, it's good that I did. It gave me time to learn who I really am. But I did that all wrong too. I shouldn't have left you thinking you were the one who'd done something wrong. But I had to get away from you after that night, Paulie. I didn't know how to feel about what I'd done. What *we'd* done. And I couldn't face you not knowing how I felt. Hell, I couldn't even face myself. So I ran. I turned my back on you and Trevor and Jamie and I just ran. I'm sorry for that, Paulie. Please forgive me."

Paulie offered a gentle smile. "Of course, but—"

Ben raised a hand. "Let me finish." He took a deep breath, tugged his robe more tightly around himself, and finally centered his eyes on Paulie one more time.

"When I told you I was homesick for San Diego, that was only part of the truth. I was more than homesick, Paulie." He took another shuddering breath and leaned a hand against the doorframe to steady himself.

Paulie felt tears burning his eyes, but he made no move toward Ben. He made no outward sign of the emotions coursing through him. He could see in Ben's eyes the man's need to finish saying what he needed to say, and Paulie was determined to let him say it. But Paulie's heart was doing a tap dance inside his chest all the time he stood there. Even his hands were starting to shake.

He studied Ben standing there in the doorway as he had never studied another human being in his life. And all the time he studied him, he bit back a dawning happiness inside. For he already knew what Ben was about to say. He knew it beyond a shadow of a doubt.

And at last, Ben said the words Paulie knew—Paulie *prayed*— were coming. "I wasn't just homesick, Paulie. I was—I was too far away."

"From home?" Paulie asked, still knowing, still waiting to hear the words.

"No." Ben gave his head a sad little shake. "No, Paulie. Too far away—from you."

AT THAT moment, Paulie realized his own truth for the very first time. It was a simple truth—one he should have spotted long before tonight. But how could he? He had not known who Ben truly was. He had not known the secret Ben had been grappling with during those years at college. Perhaps if Paulie had known, he could have helped Ben come to a quicker realization about himself—a quicker acceptance of the fact he was gay. Or perhaps Paulie's interference would have only confused Ben more.

Sometimes these personal realizations can only be arrived at alone. Just as Ben had finally arrived at his.

But Paulie hadn't simply *arrived* at his own realization. It had slapped Paulie squarely in the face, jarring him all the way down to his toes. He felt as if only now, only at this very moment, was he finally waking from the dream—or the nightmare—he had been living in for the past five years. Through college. After college. That dream—that unfulfilled *need*—had been gnawing away at his every waking thought and his every sleepy imagining, yet he hadn't even known it was there. Not really.

And only now did he begin to see that what he had been secretly praying for—so secretly, in fact, he didn't even know he was doing it—well, maybe, just maybe it wasn't a dream after all. Maybe it could truly happen.

How can one man be so blessed? Paulie suddenly asked himself, swallowing a sob. *What have I ever done to deserve the blessings I've received?*

Ben stared at Paulie through eyes so filled with pleading that Paulie could not tear his own eyes away from their depths. It was as if he had lost his footing, and stumbling forward, had simply been swallowed whole by Ben's heavenly brown eyes.

As Paulie watched, spellbound, Ben licked his lips and once again, as he had so many times through the course of every single day, he pushed the hair off his face, tucking it back out of the way.

Paulie stood stunned by the emotion on Ben's face, not even cognizant of what he was about to say. Just knowing he needed to break the silence, break the tension, knowing he needed to bring some *sound* into the room.

"Maybe you should get a haircut," he muttered senselessly.

Ben frowned. "Say something real," he said, dropping his hands to his sides. "Please. After what I just told you, say something real, Paulie. Tell me I'm not making a fool of myself."

And at that, the sob, just a tiny one, escaped from Paulie's throat. His vision blurred with tears. He felt his heart stutter inside his chest, and before he knew what he was doing, before he even *thought* about what he was doing, he flung himself across the room and wrapped Ben in his arms.

As Paulie held him, Ben stood limp. When Paulie leaned away just enough to look into Ben's face, he saw tears sliding down Ben's cheeks too. Paulie reached up and wiped the tears away with his thumbs. "You're not making a fool of yourself. Don't ever think that." And leaning forward, Paulie very softly touched his lips to Ben's.

Paulie held the kiss for only a moment. But in that moment, in the taste of Ben's kiss, Paulie remembered everything from that night two years earlier when Ben had given himself to Paulie. Paulie remembered every taste, every gasp, every utterance. The images assailed him one right after the other.

When he pulled away from the kiss, which had not been one of hunger, but of compassion and understanding, Paulie saw that Ben's eyes, behind damp eyelashes, were closed tight. As he watched, Ben's eyes slowly opened and focused on Paulie's face.

"Scope," Ben murmured.

"What?"

"You taste like Scope. Mouthwash."

Paulie faked a laugh, because a real laugh simply wasn't in him at that moment. "Trust me, it's preferable to what I would have tasted like *before* I gargled."

Ben answered with a smile, but the smile never reached his eyes.

"What are you thinking, Paulie?"

Paulie didn't hesitate. "I'm thinking how much I've missed you. I'm thinking how much my life just seems to stumble along when you're not around. I'm thinking my heart has to be very careful here. But I'm also thinking I don't care if it's careful or not. Does that answer your question?"

One last tear slid down Ben's cheek. This one Ben wiped away himself. He reached up to bury his fingers in Paulie's hair. Gently. Caressing.

"My own heart doesn't *want* to be careful any more, Paulie. It's been careful long enough. Tell me I can spend time with you. Tell me we can get to know each other again. Tell me I don't have to be afraid of saying or doing the wrong thing. Tell me I can be myself, my true self. Tell me you'll let me do all that, Paulie. I want to make up for the hurt I caused you. But most of all I—I just want to be with you for a while."

Paulie dropped his head to Ben's chest. He closed his eyes when he felt Ben's arms wrapping around him, enfolding him, pulling him close.

Hoarse with emotion, Paulie whispered, "I've never wanted anything else but to be with you."

"Come to bed then," Ben cooed, his lips in Paulie's hair. "Let me hold you. Just hold you."

"Yes," Paulie sighed, his pulse thundering in his ears. "Yes."

Chapter 10

PAULIE FELT a tremor in his hand as he rested it on Ben's arm. They were so close he could feel the stirring of the air from Ben's breath, could smell the soap Ben had bathed with after dinner.

They were so close he could see an errant eyelash resting on Ben's cheek. He reached up and brushed it away.

"Your room or mine?" Paulie shyly asked, as if it was a matter of great importance.

Ben gave Paulie the same look he might have bestowed upon the one blithering idiot in a roomful of geniuses. "Paulie, it doesn't matter."

"I knew that," Paulie muttered, feeling the heat rise to his neck.

Ben pretended to smile, but he was obviously too nervous to try very hard. He took Paulie's hand and led him from the bathroom to Paulie's bed. Without releasing Paulie's hand, he sat at the edge of the mattress and gazed up at Paulie standing before him. When Paulie just stood there like a numbnuts because he wasn't exactly sure what Ben wanted him to do, Ben clucked his tongue and pulled Paulie down to sit beside him.

Still in their robes, they sat side by side, still holding hands. The room was half-dark, lit only by the light spilling through the bathroom door.

"Lay beside me," Ben said, and clutching their robes primly around them so that no jiggly parts fell out, they lay back on the bed, squirming around until they were comfortable and close together. When they were side by side, facing each other from across the same pillow, Paulie pulled Ben into his arms.

Ben sighed as he snuggled in. "This feels good."

"I know it does."

After a moment of blissful silence, Ben said, "There's a lump at the foot of the bed."

"That's Hammer. Just work around him."

"Okay."

Ben snuggled his face into the crook of Paulie's neck and closed his eyes at the sensation of Paulie's hands stroking his back. His own hand, the one he hadn't tucked under the pillow, he slipped beneath the collar of Paulie's robe and rested on Paulie's warm, bare shoulder. He felt his cock immediately lengthen at the feel of Paulie's skin against his fingertips, but he ignored it. He hoped Paulie would ignore it too, if he noticed. This was not the time for sex. Ben needed something other than sex right now. He needed—Paulie. Paulie's closeness. Paulie's heat. Paulie's *presence*. He hoped Paulie would understand that.

And apparently, Paulie did.

When Paulie spoke, his voice was little more than a susurration of sound. The merest of whispers. A tiny ripple of noise that barely traveled through the shadows to Ben's ears. "Oh God, Ben, you have no idea how long I've wanted to feel you in my arms like this. Since the day I met you, I think. That day when we were signing up for— whatever class it was."

"Poetry," Ben whispered back, his breath sweet and warm against Paulie's cheek. "Haikus and Shit 101."

"Haikus and Shit 101," Paulie echoed with a smile, remembering the nickname they had dubbed the class they both hated. "That's right. Freshman year. We were both nervous, didn't know what the hell we were doing."

At that, Ben chuckled. "Still don't." He was obviously referring to the awkward way they had come together on this oddly wondrous night.

Paulie chuckled back. He couldn't agree more. "Seems that way, doesn't it?" And then, Paulie added what he knew to be the truth. "If you hadn't taken the bull by the horns tonight, we still wouldn't."

Ben tensed in his arms.

"What?" Paulie asked. "What's wrong. What did I say?"

Ben pressed his face into Paulie's neck, breathing in the scent of him. When he spoke, he could feel his lips moving against Paulie's skin. It felt amazing. He could also feel the blood rushing to his face as Paulie's arms tightened around him.

"Those were the words I used that night, Paulie. Something about the rich boy finally taking the bull by the horns. I don't know how I remember that. I was drunk as a skunk."

Paulie smiled, remembering. "We both were. Yet I remember everything about that night. Everything. You told me to toot your horn and play you a song. Your horn was really your—"

"I know what my horn was." Ben giggled. Then he broke into laughter and buried his face even deeper in the crook of Paulie's neck. Paulie's collarbone was hard against his mouth. He liked feeling it there. Sexual thoughts of Paulie, both old memories and new imaginings, invaded his thoughts even as he grew red with embarrassment from remembering that stupid line about Paulie tooting him a song.

"I was an idiot," Ben said.

"You were beautiful," Paulie answered, his voice breathless with the truth of his words.

Ben lifted his head to gaze up at Paulie. He could see Paulie's eyes and teeth sparkling white in the darkness. He was smiling.

"Was I?" Ben asked.

Paulie smiled all the wider, tilting his head down to gaze back at Ben's upturned face. "Was and still are. You're the most beautiful man I've ever seen. When you were born you managed to acquire every right gene there is to acquire. When your DNA came together it was a perfect storm of genetic creativity. God pretty well fucked everybody else up in one way or the other, but you he got right. You should send him a thank you card."

"I'll try to remember."

"Sarcasm," Paulie said, pulling Ben's head back down to his chest. "Very unappealing."

"See? I'm not perfect after all."

When Ben looked up, Paulie kissed the tip of his nose. "I guess not."

A silence fell that was broken only by the sound of Hammer snorting himself awake. He dragged himself out of the tangle of bedclothes, looked around as if wondering where he was and how the fuck he had gotten there. Then he gave himself a shake, and leapt off the bed, heading for the door.

"I guess we were disturbing his ass," Paulie said.

"Guess so," Ben agreed.

After a heartbeat of silence, Paulie asked, "Does your family know about you coming out?"

Ben burrowed into Paulie's neck again, as if hiding his face from the world. "Please, Paulie, don't bring them up right now. I don't want them inside my head. Not tonight. This night belongs to us. Me and you. I don't want to share it with anybody else. Can you—can you understand that?"

Paulie buried his fingers in Ben's thick mop of hair. Petting. Comforting the man, he hoped. Comforting himself as well. He knew Ben's relationship with his parents had always been a troubling one. And Ben was right. Paulie didn't want them intruding on this night either. It really did belong to the two of them. No one else.

He felt Ben's lips drag a tender kiss across his collarbone. Paulie closed his eyes at the moist heat of it. "Yes," he said. "I understand, Ben. I'm sorry."

Again a silence fell. Paulie sensed Ben's need to talk. Ben's need to hash things out.

"Was coming out hard?" Paulie asked. "Was it traumatic?"

Paulie felt Ben's lips smile against his skin. "Not really. Once I faced the truth about myself, it seemed to be the only natural progression I could make with my life. You did a bang-up job setting the stage for me and showing me what it was I really wanted. Every day I remembered that short time we spent together in each other's arms, and every day those memories made me hungry to experience them again. The only problem I had with coming out, with having sex with other men, was that...."

A silence fell. It lasted so long, that for a second, Paulie thought Ben had slipped into sleep. Then he realized he was searching for the right words. Being a writer, Paulie figured he would help him find them. After all, words were his life. Or so he kept telling himself.

"What?" Paulie softly asked. "Were you shy? Were you afraid? Do all the men in Nebraska dress like rubes and smell like hog poop?"

"No," Ben said, smiling and stroking Paulie's bare shoulder beneath the bathrobe. Reading braille. Reading Paulie with his fingertips. "The truth is I was disappointed."

"Disappointed? Why?"

Ben lifted his face enough to rest his forehead on Paulie's chin. Paulie could feel Ben's eyelashes fluttering against his skin, even as he dragged his own toes through the hair on Ben's shin, all but closing his eyes at the eroticism of that simple act. He felt a little exhalation of Ben's breath stir the hair on his chest.

Ben lifted his head to see Paulie's face. "I was disappointed because none of them was you, Paulie." And here Ben smiled. Self-deprecating. Resigned. He gave his head a little shake as if still not believing the truth himself. "Can you believe it? I was disappointed because none of them was you. They didn't even come close."

"Ben—"

"I think you ruined me for other men, Paulie. It's the only way I can explain it. Does that put you on an ego trip?"

"No." Paulie grinned. "But it pleases the shit out of me."

"Lovely expression."

"Thank you."

Paulie touched his lips to Ben's forehead in a gentle kiss. Just before pulling away, just before breaking the kiss, Paulie brushed the tip of his tongue over Ben's flesh. When he did, they both closed their eyes at the sharing of such a tiny sliver of intimacy.

Paulie savored the taste of Ben's skin on his tongue as he wondered if he should say what he was about to say. Finally he decided he couldn't *not* say it. "I guess we're both ruined, then, because I haven't been happy with a trick since the day I ravaged you."

"Was I a trick?"

Paulie pushed Ben back to better see into his eyes in the dim light. "No! Don't ever think that! You were the pinnacle, for Christ's sake. You were Mt. Everest. You were that one special conquest that defined my life, Ben. You defined—*me*. Hell, you've *always* defined me, I think. Even before that drunken night, I thought of very little else but you. You were a dream for me. Something to aspire to and wish for and know that, ultimately, I would never attain. Until tonight. When you told me you were gay. Now maybe...."

"Maybe what, Paulie?"

Ben's face was open and eager, his eyes wide. Piercing. Paulie's heart shuddered gazing into them. *Tumbling* into them.

"Nothing, Ben. It's nothing."

Ben squeezed his eyes closed and again rested his forehead on Paulie's chin. "No, Paulie. Don't let it end like that. Tell me what you were about to say."

"I'll scare you off. I just got you back, and I'll turn right around and scare you off again. I'm not going to say it. Not tonight. All right?"

Ben nodded as if he understood. He didn't like it, but he understood. Again he lowered his head to press his lips to Paulie's collarbone. "All right."

Paulie clutched Ben tighter in his arms. He pushed his face into Ben's thick, fragrant hair, inhaling the scent of it, letting it billow across his face. He felt their bare knees bump against each other. The hair on their thighs scraped together. Their robes were slipping. Paulie's cock was so hard it ached, and for the first time he realized Ben was hard too.

A sudden avalanche of desire for the man tore through Paulie's body. Once again he remembered everything about that night so long ago—the way Ben's cock tasted on his tongue, the length and girth of him, the heft of his balls, the way he trembled and arched his back just before he came. In torrents.

But this was not then. This was tonight. Paulie bit his lips against the current urges and the age-long memories and concentrated on the words Ben had spoken tonight. *Let me hold you. Just hold you.* If that was what Ben wanted, it was the least Paulie could do. The very least.

But maybe—just maybe—it wasn't what Ben wanted after all. Not really.

Ben's warm mouth found the hard nubbin of Paulie's Adam's apple. His lips foraged there for a moment, then worked their way up to Paulie's jawline.

"You need a shave," Ben muttered.

"Sorry."

"No. I like it."

Paulie felt a tremor run through him as Ben's lips found Paulie's earlobe. Ben sucked it into the wet heat of his mouth, and Paulie trembled again. Ben's hand slipped from his shoulder and buried itself in Paulie's armpit. His fingertips moved through the hair there. Then those heavenly fingers slid south over the warm wales of Paulie's ribcage.

Paulie could feel a shudder run through Ben's body as they nestled together. *Christ,* Paulie thought, *we're quailing and quaking like we've got malaria.* Things were getting out of hand, and he knew it.

Paulie pressed his lips to the side of Ben's bristly neck. Ben needed a shave too. Just like he did. The heat and smell of Ben's skin was driving Paulie crazy. Actually, it was Ben's broad, warm hand on his ribcage that was really fueling the hunger. Paulie wanted that hand to keep moving. Keep moving. The bristly heat of their thighs rubbing together wasn't helping matters either.

"You said you wanted us to just—you know—hold each other," Paulie stammered, hating himself for saying the words. Hell, what if Ben backed off? That was the *last* thing Paulie wanted.

But Ben seemed to have no intention of backing off.

His tongue had found Paulie's ear canal, and Paulie's toes were starting to curl as that wet tongue burrowed in, beginning a gentle exploration. In a voice hoarse with need, Ben whispered, "I know what I said. I'm beginning to reassess the situation."

"Oh. Good."

Without warning, Ben pulled away completely. Paulie grabbed his arms. He was struck by the terror that Ben was going to go brush his teeth again. Or worse, go back to his own bedroom and close that fucking door for the night. "No, Ben! Don't go!"

Ben eased himself from Paulie's grasp and stood at the side of the bed looking down at him.

Paulie's eyes had adjusted to the darkness now. The bathroom light was more than enough to show him everything he needed to see. He watched, spellbound, as Ben slowly unknotted the cloth belt around his waist and slipped the robe off his shoulders. It slid down his back, landing in a heap at his feet.

Paulie raised himself up on his elbows to take in the beauty of Ben standing naked and hard before him.

Ben laid a hand over his erect cock and pushed it down, as if to hide his nakedness, but Paulie uttered, "No," and Ben moved his hand. His cock sprang up. Paulie could see a glimmer at the tip of it where a drop of precome sat glistening, catching the light.

"Oh Jesus," Paulie muttered.

Ben stood trembling before him, offering himself completely. When he spoke, his voice was barely a croak.

"You wanted me once, Paulie. Do you still want me?" There was a pleading in his voice that tore at Paulie's heart. *How can you conceivably think otherwise?*

Paulie reached out and caressed Ben's knee. It lay hard and trembling beneath his palm. "Yes, I still want you, Ben. I've never stopped wanting you. Christ, haven't you figured that out yet?"

A tiny smile lit Ben's face as he stared down from the shadows. "That's good, Paulie, because I know now that I want you too. No tricks this time. No bullshit. No trying to be anything other than who and what I am. I want to be honest with you this time. I want to just— be myself."

Paulie tore his eyes from Ben's cock and gazed up at Ben's downturned face. "You being yourself is all I've ever wanted, Ben. You being yourself is more than enough for anyone to ever want."

Ben stretched out his hand, and Paulie gave a tiny gasp when that hand headed straight for his crotch. But at the last moment, it simply gripped the belt of Paulie's robe and tugged it loose.

"Take it off," Ben said, his voice hushed. "Let me see you."

With his eyes still centered on Ben's face, Paulie shrugged out of the robe and raised his hips to slide it out from under himself. When he was free of it, he flung it in a corner and dropped his head back to the pillow, hands behind his head, his erect cock moving almost imperceptibly to the rhythm of his heartbeat as he lay on his back, legs flung wide, hiding nothing. Paulie's heart was pounding so hard, he wondered if Ben could hear it.

Ben rested a knee on the edge of the bed. He reached down and slid his fingers through Paulie's thick blond hair and over his cheek. Then he let his fingertips trail over the soft, firm skin of Paulie's underarm, lingering at the bicep, obviously relishing the firmness of it. The *perfection* of it.

Ben's voiced was stunted with emotion. A husk of sound in the darkness. "I told you I remember everything about that night, Paulie. And I do. But the memory that has torn at me for the past two years and won't let me go, is how I did nothing to give back what you were giving me."

Paulie untucked his hand from behind his head and pulled Ben down to sit beside him. When their hips were touching, skin upon skin, Ben's hand came to rest on Paulie's stomach. At the same moment, Paulie's hand came to rest in the scattering of hair on Ben's chest. Paulie's whole body trembled at the first touch of it.

It took every ounce of Paulie's willpower to leave that hand where it was and try to speak coherently at the same time. But he knew what he wanted to say, and that helped.

"You didn't give back to me, Ben, because you were still confused about who you were. I understood that then, and I understand it now. It's a wonder you gave back as much as you did, the way I took advantage of the situation."

Ben's hand slid over Paulie's belly button. Ben rested a fingertip inside it, and it was all Paulie could do not to raise his hips off the bed.

"I won't make the same mistake twice," Ben said. "I've dreamed of doing this since I first understood what my feelings about you were."

And before Paulie could respond, before he could ask what those feelings were, Ben lowered his head and placed a tender kiss on Paulie's stomach. Ben raised himself to a sitting position once again as his hand came up to cup Paulie's balls. This time Paulie's hips did come off the bed. He watched in wonder as a smile lit Ben's face and that glorious hot hand came up to circle Paulie's dick. Ben stood it upright and gave it a slow, gentle stroke.

Paulie watched as Ben licked his lips. Their eyes came together for one brief glance before Ben lowered his head and slid his tongue over Paulie's slit, licking away the drop of moisture that had accumulated there.

Ben lowered himself into the space between Paulie's outflung legs and stretched out his long body. Still holding Paulie's cock erect, he kissed his way down the hard shaft until he pressed his mouth into Paulie's balls, tasting the heat of him and smiling all the while he did it.

With Paulie's eyes never leaving his face, Ben once again slid his tongue along the shaft of Paulie's cock, over the heavy veins to the corona. At the summit, he dragged his tongue deliciously over Paulie's moist slit once more, and then he slid Paulie's cockhead into his mouth. Paulie could feel his glans expand at the sudden heat, that glorious wet heat, and with his cock buried deep in Ben's mouth, he watched as Ben's eyes traveled up to his face. They stared into each other's eyes as Paulie thrust his cock into those welcoming lips. Ben's eyelids were heavy with lust. Paulie could tell he was loving every stroke of it, every taste, every shudder.

Before thirty seconds had passed, Paulie could feel the muscles in his legs and ass tensing and jumping as if he had just run a marathon.

Ben's mouth felt spectacular.

Paulie wrapped his legs around Ben's shoulders, opening himself up to him even more.

Ben released Paulie's cock and it slapped wetly against his stomach as Ben lifted Paulie's legs, pressing his face once again into Paulie's fuzzy balls and licking his way between those firm nuts until his tongue found the beginning of all-new territory to explore.

Ben rose up onto his knees in the bed as he lifted Paulie's legs higher, and Paulie gave a gasp as that hot mouth descended on his sphincter. Ben's lips caressed him there, tasting, prodding, and when Ben's tongue slid across his opening, Paulie cried out and grabbed Ben's head.

"Oh Jesus," Paulie gasped. "Oh Jesus. You've learned a few things since the last time we were together."

At that, Ben laughed and pulled his mouth from Paulie's opening. He squirmed around on the bed until he was facing the opposite direction from Paulie. Once he was there, in a proper sixty-nine position, Paulie happily wrapped his arms around Ben's waist while Ben did the same to him. Paulie pulled Ben close until that heavenly hard cock was pressed firmly against his face. Ben's pubic hair tickled his chin, and Paulie felt another drop of precome smear across his cheek when Ben uncontrollably pressed his cock to Paulie's face.

"I'm home," Paulie muttered, as he slipped Ben's iron cock into the heat of his mouth, taking it in as far as he could while Ben thrashed and sucked in air at the sensation of that hot mouth swallowing him whole.

Ben's own mouth descended once again on Paulie's cock, and Paulie pushed his hips into Ben to help it get there. With hands everywhere and tongues stroking and circling each other's glans, Paulie tasted Ben's juices yet again as more precome seeped from his dick.

Paulie was dripping too. He could feel it. And when Ben murmured, "Delicious," he knew Ben could taste it.

Somehow that knowledge sent Paulie over the edge. Or maybe it was more than that. Maybe it was the years-long waiting and the wanting and the belief that this would never happen again, and yet somehow it had, that made Paulie give in to what his body demanded.

It was too soon, dammit, too soon. He knew that. But he could do nothing to stop it. He cried out in apology as his hips flew off the bed and the come surged from his cock. And with Paulie muttering, "Oh shit, oh Christ, oh crap," his hot come splattered the roof of Ben's eager mouth, slipped through Ben's lips to dribble down Ben's chin, and still Ben would not release him.

He drew every drop of come from Paulie's cock until there was nothing left to reap, and when Paulie shivered in completion and returned to concentrating his attentions on Ben's cock, which was once again buried to the hilt in Paulie's eager mouth, it was Ben's turn to let loose.

Ben's hand flailed and hit the wall with a bang as his come exploded out of him at Paulie's urging. His juices surged into Paulie's hungry mouth, and as they shot forth, Paulie grabbed Ben's ass, pulling him close, clinging and sucking for all he was worth, more turned on than he had ever been in his life. Wanting everything—everything Ben had to offer. With Ben's hot stomach pressed to his chest and Ben's firm balls slapping his forehead, Paulie drank down every drop of Ben's come. It was sweet and thick, like heavy cream, and Paulie smiled around Ben's cock as the man pumped and pumped and all but wept, breathless and uninhibited. It was the most beautiful thing Paulie had ever witnessed.

Finally, with a cry of astonished fulfillment, Ben relaxed his arching spine and fell back onto the bed, spent. Paulie collapsed on top of him, his face to Ben's stomach, his mouth alive with the taste of Ben's come, still hungry for more.

The two of them gave a final shudder and clutched each other close. Paulie buried his face in Ben's tangled pubic hair, drinking in the scent of him, feeling Ben's cock, hot and moist, softening against his cheek, feeling his own heart still hammering away inside his chest like a blacksmith pounding on a fucking anvil.

Ben, too, pressed his face to Paulie's crotch, inhaling him, breathing him in. When Ben spoke, his words were shuddery and weak.

"That's the way it's supposed to be," Ben panted, his voice a fractured whisper.

Paulie nodded, snuggling closer, his own voice not yet capable of uttering sound. But he knew Ben was absolutely right. *This is exactly the way it's supposed to be.*

Chapter 11

THEY FOUND each other again just as the light of dawn began seeping into the room. Half-asleep, their lovemaking was less hurried this time, yet more sweetly intense than it had been earlier. When they came, simultaneously and laughing with the gentle release of it, they held on tight, marveling at the needful beauty of that one fulfilling moment. When their hearts had thudded down to a normal cadence, they once again folded themselves into each other's arms. They were asleep before the taste of their juices had dissipated from their lips.

The next time Paulie opened his eyes, the room was awash with sunlight. Ben was lying flat on his back, one arm flung high above his head, the other dangling over the side of the bed. Paulie had his nose buried in Ben's fuzzy armpit and his hand lay atop Ben's sleep-warm chest. He thought he had never awakened in a more wonderful place in his life.

Ben was snoring like a locomotive. Paulie smiled, listening to him.

There were no bedclothes on top of the bed. They were lying naked on the bare sheet. When Paulie pressed his lips to Ben's ribcage, Ben stirred, rolling toward him. Ben's strong arms pulled Paulie snug against him as he buried his face in Paulie's hair.

"Thank you," Ben whispered.

"Thank you back," Paulie whispered in answer.

When someone other than the two of them cleared his throat not more than six feet away, Ben and Paulie bolted straight up in bed.

Jamie and Trevor had scooted the red leather chairs away from the fireplace and positioned themselves at the foot of Paulie's bed. The two were sitting there for all the world like a pair of moviegoers waiting for the previews to end and the featured attraction to begin. Trevor was licking the butter off of a scone, Jamie nibbling at a bunch of grapes.

Paulie lunged over the side of the bed and grabbed the blanket, which was jumbled up in a pile on the floor where either he or Ben had kicked it sometime during the night. He flung the blanket over their naked bodies, and only then did he scream to high heaven, "What the fuck do you idiots think you're doing? Don't you have any sense of decorum? Doesn't anyone's privacy mean anything to you at all?"

When Jamie and Trevor simply stared back at him, all innocence and wounded surprise, Paulie looked to Ben for backup. What he saw was Ben gazing at the three of them—Paulie, Jamie, and Trevor—one after the other, with a goofy grin on his face. He was as red as a rose, but he was laughing too. He seemed to find it amusing.

Paulie didn't. He turned back to the morons at the foot of the bed. "How long have you two been sitting there?"

"Clearly, not long enough," Trevor said.

Jamie agreed, "A heads-up would have been nice. I would like to have caught the show." He gazed around at the bedclothes scattered all over the room. "You two certainly know how to tear up a bed."

Trevor gazed at Jamie sitting in the chair beside him. "I'm afraid you're missing the crux of the matter, darling." He turned back to Paulie and Ben. "What I'd like to know is: why is my best straight friend having a romantic naked cuddle with my best gay friend, and if one of those two entities is my best straight friend, then why the fuck is he having a gay naked cuddle *at all* with *anybody* of the male persuasion?"

Paulie and Ben were still sitting up in the middle of the bed, but at least their private parts were chastely tucked away under the crumpled-up blanket.

Ben smiled an easy smile at Trevor's quizzical expression and laid his head on Paulie's shoulder.

"Sorry," he said. "Didn't know I was gay until I hit Nebraska. Always suspected it, of course, but wasn't sure beyond a shadow of a doubt until I landed in the Midwest. Funny how the Midwest has a way of bringing out the best in people."

"You bet," Paulie attested. He was calming down. "The *absolute* best."

Jamie watched the two of them with a dawning light in his eyes. "If you don't mind my saying so, you two look awfully cozy sitting there with your hair sticking up all over the place. If I didn't know better, I'd say you've been doing a bit more than cuddling. More intrusive things, quite possibly, judging by the satisfied smirks on your faces. What do you have to say to that?"

"It's none of your business," Paulie said, grinning, no longer angry, just resigned. The grin pretty much answered the question, though, and Jamie and Trevor knew it.

Paulie's grin spoke of something else as well.

"Holy cow, you're an item, aren't you?" The words came from Trevor, and it wasn't truly a question. "You two are nuts about each other. I can see it on your faces."

"So?" Ben asked.

And when he said it, Paulie whipped his head around to stare at Ben. He did it so quickly Ben felt impelled to lift his head from Paulie's shoulder and stare back.

"Are you saying he's right?" Paulie asked. "Are we an item?"

Ben pushed his hair out of his eyes, then he reached over and pushed *Paulie's* hair out of *his* eyes. "Only if you want to be," he answered.

"Shit yeah," Paulie said.

Ben studied his face for a couple of heartbeats. There was a gentle warmth in his eyes that melted Paulie's heart. Then a hint of a smile brought Ben's dimples into play. "Shit yeah? Every time you open your mouth, you positively exude romance. You know that? Anyone could easily tell you were a writer just by the artful way you play with the English language."

Paulie blushed. "Thank you."

Finally, Ben turned to Jamie and Trevor. "There you have it," he said. "By unanimous decision, the writer and I are indeed an item."

"Holy fucking crap," Trevor stated.

Jamie chimed in with, "Ditto with what Trevor said."

They both looked shell-shocked.

Suspecting the amazed look on his two friends' faces was remarkably similar to the one on his own, Paulie couldn't restrain himself a moment longer. He flung himself into Ben's arms, not giving two raps about the people looking on. He pulled him close and pressed his lips to Ben's smiling mouth. They closed their eyes and fell back on the bed still wrapped in each other's arms.

"Ooh," Jamie said. "Now it should get good."

Never breaking the kiss or opening his eyes, Ben pointed first at Trevor, then at Jamie. Then he aimed his finger at the door and wiggled it commandingly.

"Looks like they want us to leave," Trevor said.

"Well, shoot," Jamie said. "Might as well go, then. Maybe we should go see what Jack and the househunk are up to. I'm sure *they* know how to put on a show."

"Ooh, yeah," Trevor grinned, popping the last of his scone in his mouth. "We'll do that, then."

And a moment later, Ben and Paulie heard the bedroom door click closed. They were once again alone. Only then did Ben open his eyes and gaze into Paulie's face.

"Did you mean what you said?" Ben asked. "Don't you think it's a little soon to be calling ourselves an item?"

"Why? I've known you for years. I've wanted you for years. I've been crazy about you for years. Doesn't feel too soon to me."

"Me either." Ben smiled, and lying back on the bed, he flung the blanket aside and ran his hands over Paulie's body. "Besides, we're not picking out curtains and china patterns. We're simply declaring ourselves interested."

"Interested," Paulie echoed, snuggled up next to Ben and writhing under his touch. "Really, really interested." He buried his face in Ben's chest, listening to his heartbeat. Listening to his *own* heartbeat.

Listening to their two heartbeats together. "You got any more tricks up your sleeve you learned in Nebraska?"

Ben laughed. "I just might."

"Oh, good," Paulie said, his voice already growing hoarse with lust. "I think I'm going to like us being an item."

"Then prove it," Ben said with a wicked smile.

So Paulie did his level best to do exactly that.

HOURS LATER, with the sun high in the cobalt California sky, it was hunger that finally drove Paulie and Ben from their bed. After a joint shower, during which they found several new ways to enjoy each other's bodies, they dressed and headed downstairs to join the throng.

After the way they awoke, with Jamie and Trevor watching their every (naked) move, Paulie and Ben knew they had very little left to hide. So they decided to hide nothing.

Especially from each other. "No tricks, no bullshit," Ben had said. Honesty. And being honest meant not pretending to be anything they weren't. Or pretending to feel anything they didn't feel. That's how Paulie wanted it too. Somehow he knew that's the way it would have to be, if... if....

And there Paulie forced his mind to stop. He was afraid to look too far ahead. Afraid to think too much about what it all might mean. It jinxed things, thinking too far ahead. Jinxed them every time. Paulie didn't want this... thing, whatever it was, with Ben to somehow get fucked up. It was too important. Being with this man was Paulie's *dream,* for heaven's sake. It had always been his dream. Hell, he was almost afraid to say or do *anything,* for fear of screwing it up.

Paulie still couldn't believe everything that had happened. More than anything, all he had originally hoped for with this reunion of old college chums was a renewal of Ben's friendship. And now look what had taken place! Friendship wasn't even on the table anymore. They had moved beyond friendship with their first kiss, he and Ben. Their first... touch.

In fact, Paulie suspected he and Ben had moved beyond friendship with their first glimpse of each other when Paulie answered the front gate on the night Ben arrived. They had slipped right past friendship in a matter of one or two heartbeats.

Now they were *interested.*

Paulie arrived at another astonishing conclusion the moment he stepped from his bedroom with Ben on his arm. When writers talk about lovers walking on air, Paulie had always believed it was simply a mindless and meaningless cliché. A rose-colored interpretation of the facts and little more—long on imagination and short on reality. But now Paulie wasn't so sure, since he kept having to look down at the floor to see if his feet were actually making contact with it. He did indeed seem to be floating on air, that's how elated he was.

He couldn't help wondering what other clichés would bite the dust before he and Ben were done with each other.

They found Trevor and Jamie in the kitchen. Trevor was sitting at the counter, and Jamie was standing over him, holding a fistful of raw ground round to the front of Trevor's head.

"What the hell are you doing?" Paulie asked.

Jamie turned, and when he did, he pulled his hand away from Trevor's face.

Paulie did a double take while Ben whistled. Trevor sported a magnificent black eye that hadn't been there when the two of them were sitting at the foot of Paulie's bed.

"Get hit by a bus?" Paulie finally asked.

"Worse," Trevor growled, giving his shiner a gingerly pat with his forefinger. "Your houseboy attacked me. Totally unwarranted and vicious assault. That's my story and I'm sticking to it." He elbowed Jamie, who was trying not to laugh. "Shut up, dickwad."

Ben stuck his hand on his hip like a frustrated schoolmarm. A trick he must have learned in a Nebraska classroom. "You pulled the same stunt on Jack and Jeffrey that you pulled on us, didn't you?"

Trevor gave an uncomfortable shrug. "Maybe."

"And did you catch a show?" Paulie asked. He wasn't just being facetious either. He honestly sort of wanted to know. How perverted was that?

Jamie's face came alive. "And what a show it was! Jack's legs were straight up in the air and the househunk was splitting his ass like a farmer plowing the south forty. The man should paint his dick yellow and tattoo the word Caterpillar on the side of it. That is one bigass piece of heavy equipment. Jack was in heaven, I don't mind adding. Eyes all bugged out, gasping and moaning and quivering in ecstasy. A bit humbling actually. I don't remember him going quite so apeshit on those numerous occasions when *I* plowed his south forty."

Trevor patted his arm. "There, there. Your equipment is just fine. Maybe you just need to learn how to plow better."

Jamie snarled and slapped the hamburger to Trevor's face. Trevor said, "Ow," but Jamie didn't seem to care. He was a little keyed up.

Jamie flung his words at Paulie like a barrage of artillery fire. "Then your houseboy turned around and found us sitting at the foot of the bed. Well, you can see by Trevor's poor face that things rapidly deteriorated after that. The man stopped drilling my hairdresser long enough to pop Trevor a good one before throwing us both out of their room. Manually."

"*Ex*-hairdresser," Trevor amended.

Jamie conceded the point. "Oh yeah. Ex."

"How come he only popped Trevor?" Paulie asked.

Jamie smirked. "I ducked. Trevor didn't. Although I did skin my knee as I flew through the door."

Trevor aimed his one good eye at Paulie. "The man has to go. He's a loose cannon." As an afterthought, he added, "With a really long barrel."

Paulie laughed. "I'm not firing my houseboy because you two stuck your noses where they didn't belong. Let that be a lesson to you." He gazed around, making sure the four of them were alone, then lowered his voice. "Maybe later you can tell us more. I'd kind of like to hear the tale."

"Writers love tales," Ben droned, rolling his eyes heavenward.

"Uh, yeah," Paulie mumbled. "We do. It feeds the muses."

"Yeah, right," Ben muttered. "Those altruistic muses."

Paulie innocently gazed around, seeking to snatch a change of subject out of midair. "So. Where is everybody?"

"Danny's surfing," Jamie grumped. "Jack is hopefully douching."

"The houseboy is polishing his brass knuckles," Trevor snapped.

"Oh hush." Paulie grinned. "You got what you deserved and you know it."

Trevor sneered. "Harumph."

Paulie smiled at Ben. "Breakfast?"

"You bet, babe. I'm starved."

Jamie and Trevor dropped their wounded personas long enough to give each other a sappy, romantic look after watching this little interchange between Paulie and Ben. While they might not yet know the full details of how the two had gotten together, they were obviously thrilled they had. Paulie and Ben were their best friends, after all. And only yesterday one of them was *straight*. Who wouldn't want to know the full details about *that*?

Everyone turned at the sound of footsteps to find Jeffrey, with Jack hanging on his arm like a barnacle, strolling and giggling their way into the kitchen. Apparently, they had taken Paulie's new house rules to heart before toddling down the stairs. They were both dressed.

Jeffrey parked Jack at the counter, gave him a friendly pat on the head like he might a poodle, and to be even more friendly, he bent down and stuck his tongue in Jack's ear, which one usually *doesn't* do with poodles. He waggled his tongue around until Jack was quivering in his seat. Only then did Jeffrey turn, studiously ignoring Jamie and Trevor. Instead, he chose to ogle Paulie and Ben standing there hand in hand watching him.

"Damn, Boss," Jeffrey cooed in his warm, booming voice, eyeing Ben up and down. "You did good."

Paulie blushed and squeezed Ben's hand a little tighter. "I did, didn't I?" Since he was feeling gracious and generous as all get-out, he cast his eyes at Jack, then back to Jeffrey. "So did you."

Jeffrey seemed surprised. "You mean Jack? Oh, he's just a biology experiment."

It seemed the mere rumble of Jeffrey's baritone was enough to turn Jack on. Still perched at the counter he reached up and began twiddling his nipple through the T-shirt he was wearing.

"Stop that," Jamie barked.

Trevor gave Jamie a consoling pat on the back. "He used to twiddle his tits for you. Remember?"

Jeffrey still chose to ignore the two. All smiles, he announced to Paulie, "Breakfast for the two late-to-rise gentlemen coming right up. Scrambled eggs and bacon okay? It's about all I know how to cook. I'm afraid my talents lie elsewhere."

"Do they ever!" Jack hummed.

Everyone stared at Jack for about three seconds, then went back to what they were doing.

"Bacon and eggs would be great," Paulie and Ben said in unison, pulling up stools and making themselves comfortable, their shoulders snugged up against each other, hands still firmly clasped under the countertop.

Still ignoring Jamie, Jeffrey finally deigned to speak to Trevor. It was really more of a snarl. "How about you, Snoop Boy? What would you like for breakfast? Eggs? Bacon? Another left hook?"

Trevor snarled right back, while Jamie elbowed Trevor to get his attention.

"Are you hungry?" Jamie asked.

And Trevor answered, "No."

"Can you still fuck with that eye?"

And Trevor's one good eye lit up like a road flare. "Hell yes,"

"Good," Jamie said, dragging Trevor off his stool. Two seconds later they were gone.

Jeffrey didn't seem to notice. He was rooting through the freezer. "Ooh! Look what I found!" he cried out, happy as a lark. "Tater Tots! Rich boy's got ghetto hash browns!"

Paulie blushed. "They were on sale," he mumbled to the wall.

Chapter 12

THUS BEGAN a period of Paulie's life unlike any other he had ever experienced. Not only did he have his good friends around him again, but he also had Ben. All of Ben. And he quickly found Ben to be a generous, committed partner in this sexual and emotional odyssey they had undertaken together.

But most astonishing to Paulie was the fact that the sexual part of the odyssey was in reality just a fascinating side trip on their journey of discovering each other. As wonderful as Ben was in bed, Ben's sexual generosities were only the tip of the iceberg when it came to what the man was willing to offer Paulie. He was kind, sweet, demonstrative, and a perfect listener. When he spoke to Paulie of his own feelings on the host of subjects they delved into in the process of relearning about each other, he could never be seen to hold anything back. Just as he did with his body, Ben gave of his mind completely.

And they spoke of everything. Books, music, theater, art. The way they felt in each other's arms. The way they hungered for each other every minute of every day. Their mutual preference for Fruity Pebbles over Captain Crunch with Crunch Berries. The insanity of their friends.

The only thing they did not speak of was... love. They both seemed to understand it was too soon to speak of such things. Far too soon.

The first time the word was spoken at all was in the second week of their burgeoning relationship. And it was spoken by Ben.

They were once again lying by the pool. Nude now, just as all the others were. Propriety seemed to have suffered a setback. There was no longer even an *inclination* to don swimming trunks while poolside. Even Ben wasn't immune from the freedom only nudity could bring. The most any of them donned was a towel. And a tan. And maybe a boner now and then.

Paulie lay on his stomach on a chaise lounge pretending to sleep while Ben lay on his back on another chaise lounge parked inches away from Paulie's. Ben was reading Paulie's novel, one printed page at a time. When he was finished with each page, he would carefully slip it into the box lid and pull out another from the box, assuring none would blow away on the wind.

Paulie was pretending to sleep because he enjoyed watching Ben read. He squinted through his eyelashes at Ben's naked body as it baked in the sun. Ben was tanning nicely. In only the few days he had been back, Ben had turned a luscious golden brown.

The others were clustered around the pool—Jeffrey and Jack snuggling and whispering in the shallow end as they sipped cocktails, up to their belly buttons in the water. Trevor and Jamie and Danny were sitting beneath the umbrella table playing strip poker backwards, starting nude and donning an article of clothing with every losing hand. Poor Danny was already up to wearing one sock, a baseball cap, and sunglasses. Paulie suspected his shorts would be the last thing he donned. Like the rest of them, Danny had come to enjoy the freedom of being naked. And Trevor and Jamie certainly weren't complaining. How could they? Danny was beautiful.

But not as beautiful as Ben.

While Paulie lay on his stomach on the chaise lounge, his cock hard and hungry beneath him, Ben suddenly turned to him and smiled. White teeth flashed in the sun. It was then that Ben first used the L-word. And just hearing the L-word on Ben's lips was enough to cause Paulie's pulse to stutter and his dick to grow even harder.

"I love the way you write, Paulie."

Paulie smiled back, trying to act cool while his heartbeat pounded in his ears. "Do you?" He couldn't get over how that tiny four-letter word had sounded slipping from between Ben's lips. Love.

"Yes," Ben said. "I don't have to decipher your words at all. There's a clarity about your phrasing that makes the images you try to evoke immediate and crystal clear. Only the best writers have that talent. I really do love the way you write."

And Paulie almost asked, "Is my clarity of phrasing all you love?" But he bit his tongue and left the words unsaid. When he did, a flash of discontent crossed his face, although he didn't know it.

But Ben did.

"What's wrong?" Ben asked. "What did I say?"

Paulie forced a grin and shook his head. He grabbed a towel from the deck and wiped the sweat from his eyes. "Nothing, Ben. You didn't say anything. I'm glad you love the way I write."

Ben studied Paulie's face a moment longer. A hint of a smile twisted his mouth. One dimple slowly deepened. "Your clarity of words isn't the only thing I love, you know."

"Oh yeah?" Paulie was afraid to even look at Ben now. He watched Danny and Trevor laughing at Jamie tying a bandanna around his head. He must have lost a hand.

"Yeah," Ben said. "There's other things I love too."

Paulie's pulse was thundering in his ears again. He began to wonder if Ben was tormenting him purposely. "Like what?" he asked, dragging his eyes back to Ben. Losing himself in that sweet smile of his. Losing himself too in those warm brown eyes of Ben's, almost completely hidden beneath the curtain of black hair hanging in his face. Paulie longed to climb into the lounge chair with Ben and cradle his naked body just to feel it pressed against his own. "Name one other thing you love, Ben. Just one."

If he says Tater Tots, I'll kill him, Paulie thought.

"You," Ben said. "I love you. I've loved you since my sophomore year in college, as a matter of fact. I assumed you knew." And with a secretive, smug little smile, he went back to the manuscript.

Paulie lay staring at him. Did Ben just say what Paulie thought he said? Again Paulie wiped the sweat from his eyes with the towel so he could see better. He sure as hell didn't want to miss anything.

Ben ignored him completely, seemingly engrossed once again in Paulie's manuscript.

Paulie sat up, reached over, and snatched the page out of Ben's hand.

Ben merely lay back on the lounge with his hands behind his head, naked and stunning, perusing the sky as if he didn't have a care in the world. When he started whistling a nonchalant little tune, Paulie had just about had enough.

He leapt from his chair, hard-on and all, gave Ben a shove, and tipped him and his fucking chair into the pool. A heartbeat later, Paulie dove into the water after him. They wrestled underwater while the chaise lounge sank to the bottom. In a tangle of arms and legs, they burst into the light and swung the water from their eyes.

Paulie pulled Ben into his arms as they treaded water. Their cocks were both hard now; their warm stomachs pressed tight, one against the other. Ben was laughing as Paulie sputtered after taking in a lungful of chlorinated pool water. Once Paulie had himself under control, he cupped Ben's face in his hands and held him motionless in the water.

"Say it again," Paulie said.

Ben was all innocence and confusion. "Say what?" He was trying desperately not to laugh, but failing miserably. "Say what, Paulie?"

"You know damn well what."

Ben snapped his fingers. "Oh. You mean that thing about loving the way you write?"

"No."

"You don't mean that thing I said about loving *you,* do you?"

Paulie's eyes narrowed. Once again his heart was banging and thumping away, sounding for all the world like those bigass machines buried deep in the bowels of Hoover Dam.

"Yes, Ben. That's exactly what I mean. That thing about loving me. You did say that, right? I wasn't hallucinating? I didn't dream it? You actually said it?"

"Sure, I said it. Why shouldn't I? It's true."

The only sound Paulie could hear for the longest time was the water lapping at the edge of the pool. That and the continued pounding of his heart. When he spoke, his voice was barely a whisper. His voice box seemed to have short-circuited or something. "Is it?" he asked in a hush. "Tell me, Ben. Is it really true?"

Ben leaned forward and nipped gently at Paulie's lower lip with his snow-white teeth. "You know it's true. I've loved you for years. This isn't a spur of the moment epiphany, you know. I don't do spur of the moment epiphanies. This isn't one of those instant love plots you read in romance novels either. This is a love that's been around a long time. Simmering on the back burner, as it were, waiting to explode into flame."

Paulie's vision was blurring again. He wondered if he should have his eyes checked. He liked the way those words sounded, so he softly repeated them to himself. "Simmering on the back burner. Exploding into flame."

"Yep." Ben grinned. "Simmering like crazy."

Paulie gathered Ben even closer in his arms and pressed their foreheads together. He closed his eyes, and whispered, "That's beautiful. Maybe you should have been the writer."

"Maybe I should've."

Paulie smiled. "So what you're saying is—you love me."

"Yes," Ben said. His voice deep. The humor in it muted. There was a brooding in his eyes that spoke of lust and hunger and conviction. "That's exactly what I'm saying. I love you more than anything, Paulie. And if you love me back, this would be a really good time to tell me."

Paulie opened his eyes. "You know I do."

Ben reached up and brushed the wet hair from Paulie's eyes. "Then say it for me, Paulie. I want to hear you say the words."

A profound silence had fallen around the pool, but Paulie and Ben were too engrossed in each other to notice.

Paulie sucked in a great shuddering breath when Ben slid his hand through the water between them and slipped his fingers around Paulie's stiff cock. His thumb slid back and forth across Paulie's slit, and Paulie thought if Ben kept that up for very much longer, he would come right there in the pool.

It took Paulie a moment to find his voice. He had no such problem finding the words. He knew exactly what he wanted to say. It was quite simple really. Talk about clarity of phrasing.

"I love you too, Ben. I always have. This last week has been the happiest I've ever spent on this miserable fucking planet."

Ben spit up a chuckle while his fingertips continued exploring Paulie's dick and balls. Ben was stroking him now, and Paulie's hips were moving under the water, fucking Ben's fist. His cock felt hard enough to cut glass. Ben marveled the man could talk at all.

"Don't get carried away, Paulie. You're young, you're rich, you're good looking. What's so fucking miserable about that?"

Paulie slapped himself in the head. He wasn't sure, but he thought he heard a hollow bonking sound when he did it. "You're right. I'm an ungrateful prick. It's a wonderful fucking planet. And now that I know we actually love each other, it's going to be even more wonderful." After a pause, he added, "Isn't it?"

And this time Ben really laughed. "Yes, Paulie. It is. The most wonderful planet ever."

Ben's strong arms dragged Paulie close. Their mouths came together, tongues gently seeking out the other's. Paulie buried his fingers in Ben's hair and Ben's thumb dragged a final stroke across the tip of Paulie's cock.

With a shudder and a groan, Paulie came in Ben's hand. Even under water, Ben could feel the heat of it when it splashed against his stomach. A moment later, Paulie's semen floated to the surface in globs and strings, bobbing around their chins.

Trevor, Jamie, Danny, Jack, and yes, even Jeffrey, stood at the edge of the pool and gave a standing ovation.

Jamie raised his drink in a toast to the heavens.

"I now pronounce these two nitwits lovers!" he announced, and everyone cheered. "If coming in the pool doesn't seal the deal, nothing does!"

Paulie ignored them, overcome with emotion. Clinging to Ben, and still trembling and weak from his orgasm, Paulie was too busy battling the urge to either laugh like a fool or cry like a baby. He wasn't sure which.

Misty-eyed and smiling, Ben held him tight until Paulie's laughter won the war.

"I'M SEVERING ties with my family, Paulie. If I don't sever ties with them, they will sever ties with me, and I'd rather the decision came from me."

Paulie and Ben were once again jogging along the silver strand of beach below Paulie's La Jolla mansion. It was the hottest part of the day, high noon, and since it was a weekday, they had most of the beach to themselves. A half mile back, Jamie and Trevor were swimming in the surf while Danny floated a quarter mile out on Paulie's longboard, waiting for the right swell to come along. Jeffrey and Jack were lying under a beach umbrella making goo-goo eyes at each other. And when they weren't making goo-goo eyes, Jeffrey and his "assistant" were doling out champagne and beer from a cooler Jeffrey had brought along for the purpose. Jeffrey also had a picnic basket of fried chicken and potato salad, if anyone actually decided they'd rather eat than drink, which sure as hell hadn't happened yet. Like a good little houseboy who was beginning to appreciate the finer things in life, Jeffrey had even packed the Spode and stemware.

Nothing like a gay romp on the beach with your best friends, your well-hung houseboy extraordinaire, and most of your dining room crystal to set the tone for the day.

At Ben's words, Paulie stumbled to a halt, dragging Ben to a stop beside him. "Sit down," he said. "Talk to me. What are you saying? Why would you sever ties with your family?"

They dropped to the ground, both men immediately tugging off their sneakers and ankle socks and shaking out the sand that had found its way inside.

When he was finished emptying his shoes, Ben set them aside and wrapped his arms around his knees as he gazed out at the ocean.

"My father will never accept me being gay, Paulie. And my mother will go along with whatever my father decides. You've met them. You know what they're like. The way I see it, I have two choices. I can tell them I'm gay, and when they go batshit crazy, get used to the idea of never seeing them again. Or I can *not* tell them I'm gay, and never let them know who I really am. In other words, live a lie." He turned to Paulie. "Pick one."

Paulie jumped. "Who? Me?"

"Yeah." Ben cupped Paulie's chin in his hand and smiled. "I've been thinking about this since I came out. All the way back in Nebraska. I can't decide what to do. Since you're the man I love, I'll do whatever *you* think I should do." He laughed. "Then if it's the wrong decision, I can blame you."

Paulie groaned. "Great."

Ben pushed his hair out of his face and Paulie studied him while he thought the problem over. At the moment, since he had slipped off his shoes and socks, Ben was dressed in running shorts and nothing else. For the umpteenth time, Paulie found himself lost to the world staring at him. What a knockout Ben was. Paulie had never been so in love in his life. And wonder of wonders, Ben loved him back. Paulie still couldn't believe his luck.

Eyeing Ben and all the while digging his bare toes through the hot sand because it felt good, especially to the toe without a toenail, Paulie sat there until he came to a decision on the matter.

"Don't tell them," Paulie decided. "No, wait." He thought it over a few seconds longer. "Okay. Yeah. Don't tell them. Live a lie. It's no skin off your nose. At least then you'll still have your family, although I have to admit they're a little annoying to be around. Praying all the time and shit. It must have been a real trial growing up a preacher's kid."

Ben grumped, "Tell me about it. My childhood sucked. My mother used to tell me to keep my hands above the covers when I slept so I wouldn't be tempted to touch myself. Can you believe that?" Then he grinned and bumped his head against Paulie's shoulder. "Adulthood's looking up, though. Now I don't have to touch myself."

Paulie kissed the top of Ben's head. "You got that right. That's my job."

They sat up, remembering they were on a public beach. Still sitting hip to hip in the sand, since there was nothing wrong with doing *that* on a public beach, Ben reached over and rested a hand on Paulie's arm. He tenderly stroked the blond hair there while he considered what he wanted to say. After a while he seemed to have it sorted out in his head.

"I can't live a lie, Paulie. I have to be who I am, not who they want me to be. Besides, if I do what you say, you will be excluded from the time I spend with them. How can I ask my gay boyfriend to sit down to dinner with my homophobic parents? Short answer—I can't. You are a bigger part of my life now than they are. I should be making special arrangements to include them, not you. You I love. Them I tolerate."

Paulie clucked his tongue. "You love them. You know you do."

Ben conceded the point. "Okay, yeah. Maybe a little." And then he smiled, but the smile quickly faded. "But I don't love them enough to live a lie for their benefit. I can't do it. I won't. I can live without my family if I know I have you, Paulie. And once my parents find out who I am, I will have lost them anyway. I've put up with my father's crazy religious zealotry since I was old enough to realize what a fanatic he was. It's time to draw the line on how much I let his craziness impact my life."

He sought out Paulie's eyes. "Do you understand? I don't want to be cruel to them. I just want to be myself, and the only way I can do that with my parents is from a distance. Their intolerance makes distance a necessity." He sucked in a deep breath and said what was *really* on his mind. "If they want to be a part of my life, they have to accept me for who I am, and they have to accept the man I love for who *he* is. You, Paulie. We're a package deal. At least *I* think we are. I hope you feel the same way."

Paulie touched his lips to the back of Ben's hand. "You know I do."

"Then it's settled. We're meeting them in a couple of days for lunch. We'll tell them then."

Paulie jumped again. "We?"

"Yeah. You're coming too."

"Oh goodie."

"Thought you'd like it."

Once again Ben gazed out at the water. Paulie saw sadness in Ben's eyes. But there was determination there too. And stubbornness.

Paulie knew Ben would do exactly what he said he would do. But somehow, to Paulie, it still felt wrong. You only have one family. They should be protected, held close, no matter what kind of nitwits they are. Having lost his own family, maybe Paulie was a little more sympathetic on the subject.

Together, hips and hands still touching, Paulie and Ben sat in the sand and stared out to sea. The surf roared in their ears as they squinted into the afternoon sun and felt their jogging sweat dry on their bodies.

"It'll be all right," Paulie softly said, the sea breeze lifting the hair around his face.

Ben nodded. "I'm sure it will."

They were lying and they both knew it.

Chapter 13

PAULIE WOVE his Ford through city traffic and thought about his life. Thanks to Ben, nowadays when Paulie thought about his life, his thoughts were accompanied by a smile. A big fat one.

He had a liquor list tucked in his pocket that would cost as much as most midrange cars. But what the hell. He was rich. He'd volunteered to shop for booze by himself because Ben was off on a job interview for a middle-school teaching position he had heard about, in South Park, just a few miles from La Jolla. Paulie had spent fifteen highly enjoyable minutes in Ben's crotch that morning wishing him luck.

Although his houseguests were never too lazy or busy to *drink* Paulie's booze, they did appear to be too lazy or busy to *shop* for it, which was just as well. Paulie needed some time alone anyway.

Back at the house, momentous changes in the lives of his guests were popping up daily. For instance, Paulie was stunned when he heard Jeffrey and Jack were talking about moving in together. Jack was even willing to move from San Francisco to be with Jeffrey. Apparently he *really* liked the man's big swinging dick and was more than ready to relocate his hungry ass a thousand miles down the coast to be near it.

Even more surprising was the fact Jamie had decided to move in with Trevor and Danny on his return to San Francisco. The three had become inseparable. Still, Paulie wondered how long the arrangement would last once they settled into it on a day-to-day basis. How people act on vacation is sometimes far removed from how they are willing to act every other day of the year. But so far, Paulie had to admit, the three were getting along great.

Paulie and Ben hadn't talked about moving in together, but Paulie sure wasn't going to let Ben live anywhere other than his mansion on La Jolla Beach Drive. Hell, Paulie had enough floor space to put them *all* up, but he was afraid the liquor bills would deplete even the enormous inheritance his grandmother had left him, so in four days' time, everyone but Ben had to go.

As far as Paulie was concerned, Ben would *never* go. *Ever.* Paulie wouldn't let him.

On a whim, Paulie hung a left on the freeway ramp and steered toward Mission Hills, an eclectic neighborhood of beautiful older homes and narrow winding streets. Gentrified to the hilt, Mission Hills boasted a wide array of fancy shops and expensive restaurants where San Diego's young and elite came to browse, spend their money, and sashay around looking snooty.

In the center of this bustling San Diego neighborhood sat The First Apostle's Methodist Church, a rambling limestone structure that covered half a city block. It boasted a grassy playground for toddlers on one side, and class and meeting rooms in the back behind a tall wrought iron fence. Great iron bells in the steeple high above the entrance rang out every Sunday morning, jarring the neighbors out of bed and reminding people to get their asses to church and pray away their sins. Atop the steeple stood a bronze cross, glinting brightly in the California sun.

During their college years, Paulie had been to the church on more than one occasion with Ben, who even as an adult couldn't always get out of being herded into the pews with the rest of his father's flock, for which his mother was usually responsible. She had always had an uncanny ability to play on Ben's guilts and kindnesses. Paulie and Ben had suffered through more than one god-awful hangover listening to Ben's father rant and rave from the pulpit. When Reverend Martin preached, it seemed to Paulie he left very little hope of salvation for *anybody.* Ben called his father a religious hardass, and Paulie agreed with him completely.

Even now, years later, Paulie felt hellish flames lapping at his ass and a boulder of misery settling in his gut just looking at the old church.

This morning, at the entrance of The First Apostle's Methodist Church, something new had been added since Paulie's last visit, more than two years earlier. A gigantic glass thermometer, ten feet tall, was standing by the front steps. The thermometer was sectioned off, not in degrees, but in dollars, going from zero to thirty thousand bucks. Wads of red paper had been dropped down the glass tube to depict the rising mercury. So far the mercury hadn't risen that much. The thermometer was only red between the zero at the bottom up to just short of the first one-thousand-dollar mark.

A sign at the top explained it all. With the congregation's help, amen, The First Apostle's Methodist Church was raising money for a new roof. And apparently they had a long way to go.

Paulie spit up a sad chuckle, seeing the amount they had currently raised. According to Reverend Martin's bigass thermometer, San Diego must be suffering a cold spell. And a cheap spell too. So far they had enough funds to purchase a bag of roofing nails. Maybe.

Paulie stopped his car in the middle of the street and stared at that stupid thermometer for the longest time. Then a grin began to creep across his face.

When a driver coming up behind blasted his horn and leaned out his window to scream at Paulie to "Get the fuck off the road or learn to fucking drive!" Paulie laughed out loud.

He shot the guy the finger and pulled the Ford into the first parking spot he could find. He jumped out, locked the car behind him, and headed for the church's front steps. A San Diego Gas & Electric truck was parked at the curb, along with a flood damage restoration vehicle. The door to the church was flung wide, with hoses resembling fat tube worms snaking along the sidewalk and up and over the steps leading into the vestibule. Apparently, aside from needing a new roof, Reverend Martin's establishment was suffering some sort of utility crisis as well as a major fucking flood.

Paulie explored hallways and peeked around corners, following the sound of a herd of water vacs somewhere in the bowels of the building, sucking water out of a carpet. The roar of massive fans filled the air. There were workers everywhere.

A frantic Reverend Martin spotted Paulie from the pulpit where he was in an argument with a guy in a heating and cooling uniform over the cost of a new furnace.

As if a flood weren't bad enough, it seemed the good Reverend had been slapped in the head with a perfect storm of bad luck. Apparently the church was falling down around his ears.

Such catastrophes as leaky roofs, new furnaces, and flood damage from burst water pipes were expensive undertakings.

When he thought that thought, Paulie's resolution deepened.

Tit for tat, right? Isn't that what makes the world go round?

He raised his hand and gave the good reverend a friendly wave. The man didn't know it yet, but his luck was about to change.

THEY WERE tooling down the street in Ben's Audi station wagon. Paulie and Ben sat in the front seat, with Ben driving, while Rev. and Mrs. Martin were ensconced in the backseat, trying to appear charming.

The good reverend and his wife were a little put out to learn their son had already been in the city a week and hadn't come to visit or even let them know he had arrived, but they hid it well. In truth, rather than lambasting their only son for being an inconsiderate poophead, they seemed more interested in flattering Paulie and telling him what a handsome young man he had become. Paulie knew why they were being such suck-ups, of course. Rev. and Mrs. Martin were about as hard to read as a first grade primer.

Ben was relieved by his parent's magnanimous attitude and ready forgiveness concerning his lack of courtesy in not keeping them in the loop. He was also amused and *be*mused by the way they were fawning over Paulie. The fact that the two anomalies might actually be connected had not yet occurred to him.

"There it is," Ben announced, pointing to a school complex just up ahead. "That's where I put in my application. With any luck, come September I'll be teaching seventh grade history, English, and American lit."

Mrs. Martin decided to stop sucking up to Paulie and show her son a little enthusiasm for a change. "And I'm sure you'll get the job! I know you're a wonderful teacher. It'll be so nice having you living in town again. We've missed you."

"You're not the only one," Paulie muttered for Ben's ears alone.

Ben cast him a grateful wink.

"Got something in your eye, Son?" the reverend asked, and Paulie and Ben snorted with laughter.

"Kids," Mrs. Martin cooed to the car roof, as if Ben and Paulie were nine. She smiled with resigned good humor as only a long-suffering parent knows how to do.

Mrs. Martin reached up and slid Paulie's collar through her fingertips. "Lovely shirt, Paulie."

Paulie blushed. "What, this old thing?"

And Ben snorted with laughter again.

Just down the street from the school, Paulie spotted their destination.

The Alchemy Restaurant was carefully chosen by Paulie and Ben for the evening's adventure because it was always so goddamn busy you could barely hear yourself think once you walked through the door. There was also the added consideration that Paulie was reasonably certain Ben's parents wouldn't throw a conniption fit in public once they learned why Ben had brought them here.

Ben wasn't so sure.

They were immediately seated at a table, thanks to the twenty-dollar bill Paulie tucked in the hostess's hand, an act not missed by either of Ben's parents. While they waited for their dinner menus, Ben and Paulie ordered wine, Rev. and Mrs. Martin iced tea.

Mrs. Martin had gained a few pounds since the last time Paulie saw her, but she was still an attractive lady. Her expressive brown eyes belonged to her son. She seemed a bit uncomfortable sitting in the crowded restaurant surrounded by a herd of noisy yuppies tossing down drinks. Paulie thought there just might be a bit of an inferiority complex going on beneath the woman's less-than-stylish bouffant, a fact probably due to her husband's unwavering aloofness and undying belief in his own holier-than-thou importance. It must be hard to live in the shadow of self-righteous people, Paulie decided. Not that he would ever know for sure. None of his friends quite fit that bill.

Paulie had always liked Ben's mother. Which was more than he could say of Ben's pop.

The good reverend looked exactly as he had all through Paulie's college years. Silver hair combed straight back off his lineless forehead. Icy blue eyes that sort of gave Paulie the creeps. The reverend showed a hint of Ben's beauty in the contours of his handsome face, but little of Ben's compassion. He sat now with shoulders squared, his posture ramrod straight just as it always was. Paulie thought the man looked like he had a parking meter crammed up his ass.

Ben had decided to take the bull by the horns (just as Paulie had done on that long-ago drunken night back at the apartment).

Ben was obviously in no mood to dither around. He had come to do something, and he was damned well going to do it. He downed half his glass of wine in one humongous gulp, cast a quick glance at Paulie for support, then dove right in.

"Mom, Dad, I have something to tell you."

The reverend was sipping his iced tea and trying to get the attention of the waitress. He wanted a slice of lemon. Paulie figured he could forget the lemon. He'd look sour enough in a minute anyway.

"What's that, dear?" Mrs. Martin asked, once again cooing like a pigeon.

Paulie observed her closely. He had never seen anyone self-destruct before. He thought it might be interesting to watch. Poor woman.

The reverend gave up trying to snag a waitress and turned his attention back to those sitting around him. Paulie wondered if they would have to say grace when the food came. He had never seen anyone in a restaurant do that before. Wasn't sure he was looking forward to it either. On the other hand, once Ben told them what he had to say, they might not be hanging around long enough to eat anyway.

Ben's mother rested her hand over the reverend's. Her eyes were on Ben.

"What did you want to tell us, dear?" she asked again. "Do you have a girlfriend?" This was obviously a question she had been hoping to ask for a very long time.

Paulie choked on his wine.

He choked a second time when Ben said, "In a manner of speaking, yes."

Paulie turned to him. "Say *huh?*"

Ben ignored him, but Paulie felt a commiserative foot nudge his under the table. At least he hoped it was a commiserative nudge, and not just a fucking kick for him to shut the hell up.

The good reverend seemed only mildly interested in Ben's announcement. His mother, however, was all agog. "How exciting! When do we get to meet her? What does she look like?"

Ben leaned in to the corner of the table and draped an arm around Paulie's shoulder, dragging him close. "Actually she looks a lot like Paulie. In fact, she *is* Paulie. Mom, Dad, I'm gay. Paulie and I are lovers. Don't smother us with blessings right away. We get embarrassed by effusion."

Then Ben grinned a nervous grin, and in the middle of that grin, he snatched up his wine glass and downed the rest of it. Paulie quickly did the same with his and promptly poured them both another glass. He had a feeling a little more wine would come in handy.

Ben's mom had taken a page from Lot's wife's biblical playbook and turned to a pillar of salt. All except her eyes. They kept going from Ben, to Paulie, then back to Ben. And all the time her eyes were going back and forth, her face was getting paler and paler. Suddenly her lipstick looked three shades too dark.

The reverend had not spoken a word. When the waitress came bustling over, finally, to see what he wanted, he waved her away like a gnat. She gave a huff of dismay and hustled off to appease some other ungrateful prick. She looked like she was having as bad a night as the good Rev. and Mrs. Martin.

Mrs. Martin finally tore her eyes from her son and warily cast them in her husband's direction. Her hand still rested on top of his. Paulie watched as she carefully lifted her hand and tucked it in her lap, rather like a demolitions expert might remove his hand from a particularly nasty and untrustworthy piece of ordnance he thought might explode any fucking second.

The reverend stared at Ben for the longest time while the restaurant hubbub raged on around them. They were four statues, motionless among a swirl of boisterous, cackling, yuppie humanity. The silent, unmoving eye of the storm, as it were.

And there was a storm brewing in the reverend's eye too, although it didn't show much promise of being silent. Ben's father now cast that eye on Paulie.

"You knew about this all along," he said.

Ben missed the gist of that statement. "Of course he knew about it, Pop. We love each other. Two people can't love each other if one of them doesn't know about it."

The reverend narrowed his eyes. He still stared at Paulie. Ben's brave announcement appeared to be lost among other considerations inside the good reverend's handsome head. Paulie suspected he knew exactly what those considerations were.

Finally the reverend gazed back at his son. In his shock, he seemed to have forgotten his wife's presence altogether. Paulie found himself feeling sorry for the woman. He quickly learned his sympathy was a bit premature. Mrs. Martin wasn't as helpless as he thought she was. Even wounded doves can fight back every now and then.

She threw cool words in her husband's direction. "Be careful what you say, Ralph. This is my son we're talking about too."

The reverend turned to stare at her. He blinked as if amazed by the quiet ferocity in her words.

Ben reached out to comfort his mother while Paulie decided to work on the reverend.

"Reverend Martin, your wife is right. Be careful what you say. Ben is taking the high road here. He is telling you the truth, which isn't always an easy thing to do. And he isn't telling you this truth to hurt you. He loves you both and wants you to be a part of his life. You wouldn't want to lose him over this. I know you wouldn't. And it isn't just Ben you would lose, if you turn your back on him now. You might lose *other* things."

"Are you threatening me?" Reverend Martin's voice was chilly. Dangerous.

Paulie blessed the man with an enigmatic smile. "You bet your ass I am."

"Paulie…," Ben whispered, not quite understanding what Paulie was getting at, but figuring whatever it was, it wasn't helping.

Ben's dad tensed. He opened his mouth to speak, and it didn't look like the Lord's Prayer was going to come out.

"Ralph, don't," Mrs. Martin commanded, leaning into her husband just as Ben had leaned into Paulie. She laid a small hand on his broad shoulder and gave it a pretty good shake. "It's not like we never suspected."

That statement surprised Ben. Paulie saw him jump when his mother spoke the words, but Paulie was still focused on Ben's dad. He was trying to get a point across.

"Sir, Ben loves you both the way you are. The least you can do is love him the same way. Without restrictions. He's a good person, and you should be proud to call him your son. Our sexualities don't define us. We're defined by how we live our lives. How we treat other people. Ben is a fine man, a wonderful teacher, a kind and gentle soul. I feel honored every minute of every day to know he loves me. Just as you should feel honored to have him for a son."

Ben gathered up Paulie's hand and pressed it to his lips. Ben's father looked away at the intimacy of the act, while his mother's face softened.

"And Paulie loves me just as much as I love him," Ben said, taking up the slack. "Paulie and I are together now. We're going to stay together. I hope you'll accept that. Accept *me*. I may be a disappointment to you, but I'm still your son. If you don't accept us the way we are, then I don't want your acceptance at all. You gave me life. Now let me live it the best way I see fit. If I had my druthers, I'd live it as your son. But if I have to, I'll go my way alone and never look back. But whatever happens, I stand with Paulie. I love him. I need him in my life." Ben pressed his hand to his own heart, as if trying to calm the pounding. "I'll never let him go. Not for you. Not for anyone."

Paulie was touched by the conviction in Ben's words. In fact, he wasn't entirely sure he wasn't going to start crying, he loved the man so much. Still, he didn't like the cold expression slowly growing in the old man's eyes. He had a sudden urge to leap in before the reverend said something that couldn't be taken back. Panic was growing on Ben's mother's face too. Even she knew her husband was about to say something stupid.

To avert Ben's attention from what he was about to do, Paulie pointed to the restaurant window.

"Holy cow, Ben! Look at that!"

The moment Ben turned away to stare out into the street, Paulie took the opportunity to cough into his hand. While he was coughing, he also coughed out, "Roof."

The reverend stared at him.

"I don't see anything," Ben said, turning back to the group.

So Paulie waved a frantic finger in the direction of the window *again.* "There it is! Look now! Hurry!"

Getting a wee bit perturbed, Ben once again turned to stare out the window. His mother looked too.

This time when Paulie coughed into his hand, he strangled up a few more words for the good Reverend's benefit. "Carpet!" Cough, cough. "Maybe a new furnace!" Gag, strangle, cough. Finally, in desperation, Paulie cast a brief glance in Ben's direction before spitting up his final plea. "Tit for tat goddammit!"

And with that pronouncement, Ben's father finally saw the light. He leaned forward with a hungry look in his eyes.

"Furnace?" he hissed. "Carpet?"

Paulie nodded. He wasn't sure, but he thought he saw dollar signs flash in the good reverend's eyes. Maybe he was imagining other church improvements looming in the future. If so, Paulie thought, the man would be sorely disappointed. But he could figure that out later.

When Ben turned from the window the second time, he realized the storm between Paulie and his father had somehow blown over. Even his mother looked relieved, if somewhat stunned.

The two were even more astounded when Reverend Martin extended his hand to Paulie, and sang out, "Welcome to the family, son. I hope you and Ben will be very happy together."

"Holy shit," Ben muttered, eyeing his father like he had never seen the man before in his life.

It took a second for his mother to find her voice. "Holy shit indeed," she finally echoed.

Paulie wasn't sure how much outlay of funds he had just committed to in the restoration of The First Apostle's Methodist Church, but he figured whatever the cost, it was worth it. His grandmother, after all, had left him millions. If he couldn't use a few grand to insure his own happiness and the happiness of his lover, then what the hell good was it?

Paulie hooked a friendly finger at the waitress, who immediately appeared at his elbow.

"Ready to order now?" she asked Paulie and Ben, studiously ignoring the older man who had brushed her aside earlier. Apparently, holding a grudge was a way of life with her.

"You bet." Paulie grinned, patting the waitress's hand and charming the socks off her. "My lover and I are starving. And bring us another bottle of wine, if you would."

While Paulie busied himself with the dinner orders, Reverend Martin gazed up benignly at the waitress with a blissful expression on his face. He appeared stunned by his sudden good fortune. Paulie figured lottery winners probably look the very same way.

The waitress didn't care how blissed out the old man was. She still ignored his ass completely.

Ben reached across the table and tapped his mother's wrist. "Uh, why is Dad so happy, and what the heck do you mean you always suspected?"

BEN PRESSED a finger to his lips.

Thanks to an enormous full moon beaming down from the late-night sky, Paulie could see him do it.

"Shh!" Ben hissed.

They had heard music blasting through the mansion walls when they pulled up in Ben's station wagon after safely dumping Ben's parents at their doorstep on the other side of town. Needing to be alone, at least for a while, Paulie and Ben snuck around to the back, shucked their clothes poolside, and slipped into the water.

Now here they were, naked, arm in arm in the unlit pool, savoring the feel and presence of each other and clearing their minds of the stress of the evening. It was a warm night. The dark, cool water felt heavenly. They could see Hammer's silhouette as he stood at the french doors looking out, as if wondering why they hadn't asked him to join them. While they hung on the apron, lazily treading water, Ben cuddled close and pressed his face into the crook of Paulie's neck. Paulie could feel Ben's smile against his skin. He ran his fingers over the smooth heat of Ben's strong back. The man felt so heavenly in his arms Paulie had to close his eyes for a moment to take it all in.

Ben was elated. Overall, the evening had turned out far better than he expected. He still couldn't quite comprehend his father's quick acceptance of his gayness. Paulie was elated too, although he knew that elation had cost him dearly. In the end, the good reverend had driven a hard bargain. But looking at the happiness on Ben's moonlit face as he floated there in his arms, Paulie knew the money was well spent. It was, in fact, the best (and biggest) chunk of cash he had ever dropped in his life—but it was also probably tax deductible, which eased the pain a bit. One day he might even tell Ben about it. But not tonight. Tonight was just for them. He didn't want to risk spoiling the evening, since he was pretty sure Ben wouldn't be overly thrilled by the deal Paulie had struck with his dad.

"Thanks for dinner," Paulie said around a smile. He kept his voice down. The last thing he wanted was his houseful of horny, drunken, naked guests stampeding out to join them. "You should have let your dad pay."

Ben laughed. "Well, he wasn't trying real hard to grab the check."

Paulie had to agree. "No. Check grabbing doesn't appear to be one of his faults." *Unless the check is coming from his son's rich new boyfriend and the proceeds are going to renovate his church.*

"I was proud of you tonight," Ben said, snuggling closer. "You held your own with Pop. I don't know what you two were snapping and hissing at each other about, but whatever it was, it seemed to have cleared the air nicely. Thanks."

"You're welcome. I was proud of you too. I feel so full of love tonight I think I'd sink like a rock if you let me go."

"Maybe it's just the bigass steak you consumed."

"Nope. It's love."

"In that case, I promise I won't let you go. Not tonight. Not ever."

"Good."

Their lips came together and stayed that way awhile. When Paulie was finally able to speak, he said, "Something's prodding me under the water with its hard little head. Might be a fish."

"Nope." Ben grinned. "It's my dick, but I figure you already knew that." His hand slid over Paulie's ribs, caressing, strumming. Then his fingertips slipped around to caress the cheek of Paulie's ass. One brave finger slipped into the crevice there and skidded gently over Paulie's sphincter.

Paulie shivered at the touch.

Both cocks were erect now. There were two hard-headed fish in the water.

They both glanced up just in time to spot a shooting star streaking across the sky. The beauty of it stunned them to silence.

Then Ben said, "I finished your book."

"Uh-oh."

"No, Paulie. It was really... *wonderful.* I knew you could write, but I had no idea how truly gifted you are. With every chapter I fell in love with you a little more."

"I should have made it longer, then."

Ben laughed and rested his cheek against Paulie's. This late in the day, they both needed shaves. Paulie could hear their beards scraping together.

"I was impressed, Paulie. Honest. You have to start another one as soon as possible."

"I know. I will. But not right this minute. Okay? Right now, right this very second, I have other priorities."

Ben giggled. "Does it have anything to do with our two hard-ons bumping heads under the water?"

"Maybe."

Ben pressed his lips to Paulie's ear. His words were a throaty whisper. "What is it, then? What's this big priority of yours? Spit it out. Tell me what you want." Ben's voice was sexy as hell. Just the timbre of it made Paulie's cock expand a little more.

Paulie thought about what he wanted to say for all of two seconds. Then he simply did what Ben asked. He spit it out.

"Fuck me."

"Ah. So that's it, is it?"

"Yes." Paulie's heart was already hammering wildly inside his chest.

"Here? You want me to fuck you here?"

"No. I need lubricant."

"Out of the pool, then."

"Yes. But where? I'd like to avoid the throng."

Ben thought about that. "Yes, by all means let's avoid the throng. We'll never get to our rooms unseen. How about in the cabana?"

"Good. What about a condom?"

"I have one in my wallet."

Paulie laughed. "You're kidding. What are you, fourteen?"

Ben narrowed his eyes. "You want my condom or not?"

Paulie blushed. "Well, yeah. But we still don't have any lubricant."

Ben. "I see a bottle of suntan lotion over there by that chair."

"What SPF is it?"

Ben narrowed his eyes *again.* "Does it really fucking matter? The last time I checked, the sun wasn't beaming out of your ass."

"Oh. I thought it did."

Paulie slid his lips over Ben's mouth. While they kissed and laughed, Ben's fingers circled Paulie's cock.

"That's definitely not a fish," he said.

"I didn't *think* it was."

"So *where* in the cabana?"

"On the pool table."

"You have a pool table in your cabana?"

Paulie blushed. "Well, yeah."

"Man, you *are* rich."

"You wanna fuck or bitch about the furniture?"

"Fuck," Ben said. "Definitely, fuck."

Ten minutes later, Paulie was bent over the pool table with one hand in each center pocket holding on for dear life. Ben was breathing in his ear with his dick buried to the hilt in Paulie's ass. Both men were trembling like crazy, balls were rolling everywhere, and Paulie had a smudge of blue chalk smeared across his chin.

Ben was so turned on he could barely talk. "Oh God, baby. I love billiards."

"Me too," Paulie gasped. "Me too."

Chapter 14

AFTER LYING around the pool for two weeks naked, basking in the California sun, Paulie's houseguests looked like a tribe of extremely affectionate, and possibly alcoholic, Polynesians—sunbaked to the color of filberts with not a tan line in sight.

Hammer had gained three pounds because everyone was so drunk all the time that droppage of foodstuffs had quadrupled since the old days when it was just him and his master tooling around the property. Paulie was already planning the dog's new diet, and wouldn't the poor mutt be thrilled about that?

It was the day before Trevor, Jamie, Danny, and Jack were scheduled to fly home to San Francisco. Trevor, Jamie, and Danny would be settling in together in Trevor's condo in the Castro district, and all three seemed ready and eager to dive into their new living arrangements.

Jack, of course, would be flying out with them, but then he would turn right around and drag all his belongings back to San Diego, where he would look for work here in the city after moving in with Jeffrey. This way he could also help out with Jeffrey's living expenses while Jeffrey continued his studies at Beaumont University.

Jeffrey was sorry to see the job end. These past two weeks he had spent with Paulie and Paulie's crazy friends had been the best working gig he'd ever had in his life, bar none. He was also eagerly awaiting the start of his new life with the first man he had ever had anal intercourse with who could not only happily sit right down on his leviathan nine-and-a-half-inch cock without whining about it, but then turn right around and blissfully plead for more. Jeffrey figured his big dick and Jack's accommodating ass were a match made in heaven. He even sort of loved the guy, which was an unexpected bonus. Jeffrey didn't love many people.

With all this happy turmoil and upheaval about to descend on everyone around him, Paulie was feeling a little pensive.

He and his pals were once again lounging around the pool naked, trying to soak up that last infusion of sunshine before real life intervened to put an end to their fun.

Few things suck worse than the end of vacations.

Trevor, Jamie, and Danny were frolicking in the water. Jack and Jeffrey had ducked out of the sun long enough to partake of a fuck in the sauna, as if it wasn't hot enough outside. Paulie and Ben had their lounge chairs snuggled up side by side so they could lie there and sweat in each other's arms.

Ben's fingertips were trailing a gentle path along the hard bristly ridge of Paulie's jawbone. It was morning, and Paulie hadn't shaved yet. Neither of them had. Ben's untended beard cast a dark shadow over the lower half of his face, and while it did, it also softened the upper half, bringing a light to Ben's always-gentle eyes, making the whites whiter, the brown irises warmer and more stunningly intense.

Ben's eyes were a constant peril. Paulie found himself lost in them continually. And every time those eyes centered longingly on his face, Paulie's heart gave a tiny tug like an alarm going off, warning him of the danger.

It was a danger Paulie relished.

As if Ben's eyes weren't peril enough, there was also a drop of moisture glistening at the tip of Ben's substantial erection, which Paulie longed to lick away, but there were too many eyes watching. He still had a teeny semblance of propriety left although it didn't amount to much. Even he was willing to admit that.

Paulie lay on his side with his head propped up, resting on his hand. He was gazing over at Ben who lay in the same position looking back. Paulie's free hand rested on Ben's bare hip. He wasn't entirely sure how long he would be able to keep his hand there. Already he was entertaining thoughts about sliding it just a few inches south and seeing if, with one or two lazy strokes of that magnificently uncut cock, he could increase the size of the moist little beadlet of precome oozing from Ben's urethra. He was sure he could increase it considerably if he set his mind to the task. He was even pretty sure Ben would enjoy it if he did.

He glanced down at his own cock and saw that his own drop of precome had broken free and now hung dangling from the head of his dick like an itsy-bitsy bungee cord. Apparently, Ben had noticed it too. While he watched, Ben gathered up the glistening string of precome on his fingertip and sucked it from his finger with a smile.

"Delicious," he said, smacking his lips, making Paulie's alarm go off again.

"I want you here with me," Paulie said, flat out *demanded* really, trying to ignore the quiver in his voice, which seemed to have something to do with watching Ben do what he had just done. "I want you here permanently."

"I want that too."

"I'm not talking about just temporarily. I mean always."

"I know you do."

"So you'll stay? Move in? We can be proper lovers?"

"Can I help with the expenses?"

"You can buy the lube and condoms."

Ben groaned. "I'm not sure I want to commit to *that* much fiscal responsibility. How about I just pay the property taxes, utility bills, spring for groceries, keep our cars in gas, cough up money for vet bills for your fatass dog, and swing for dental bills and medical expenses as we slowly deteriorate into old age?"

Paulie grinned. "Sure. Fine. Take the cheap way out."

They happily devoured each other with their eyes for as long as it took for Ben to scoot a little closer. He laid his palm along Paulie's cheek. They were so close he could feel the fragrant heat of Paulie's breath on his face.

"Yes," Ben said, his voice a warm promise, his words a balm to Paulie's thundering heart. "I'll stay. Wherever you are, that's where I want to be. If I look up and don't see you in the immediate vicinity, I start to panic. That precludes me living anywhere else, so I'm afraid you're stuck with me anyway."

Paulie sniffed and his eyes were burning. Maybe he was coming down with a cold. Or maybe he was just a sentimental sap who was so in love he didn't know which end was up, and every time Ben said anything the *least* bit romantic, he melted into a puddle of precome while quivering like a bowl of Jell-O.

"I'm so glad you're allergic to corn" was all he could manage to say.

Ben laughed at that, even while agreeing wholeheartedly. "Me too."

Ben scooched even closer so he could lay his lips to the tip of Paulie's nose. He even gave Paulie a little nip there with his gorgeous white teeth.

Paulie closed his eyes at the heat and sweetness of the gesture. He tilted his head back just a smidgeon so their mouths could come together in a kiss. Their tongues sought each other out. Paulie's hand circled Ben's cock at last, and Ben returned the favor.

Paulie's eyes popped open.

"No time for sex!" he snapped. "We have work to do. Let's unload that fucking U-Haul truck that's still parked at the side of the house. I'm tired of looking at it anyway. It blocks my roses."

"Faggot." Ben grinned. He twisted around to see where everyone else was. Danny, Jamie, and Trevor were lying on lounge chairs, letting the sun dry the pool water from their bodies. Jeffrey and Jack were walking naked from the sauna, their bodies shiny with sweat. Jack's ears were red and he was walking funny. Ben figured he knew what that meant. He watched as, hand in hand, they stepped right into the pool to cool off.

"What are you thinking, Ben?" Paulie asked. "You're looking devious."

"I'm thinking *we* shouldn't have to unpack the U-Haul when we have a shitload of free labor right here at our fingertips, waiting to be coerced into doing it for us."

Paulie let his eyes rove to take in everyone around the pool. "What? Them? Free labor? Are you kidding? If I showed you the liquor bills from the last two weeks, you might alter that assessment. But you're absolutely right. Let's make them pay us back for all that booze with a little hard work. Fuck 'em. They've lounged around long enough on the public dole."

Ignoring his hard-on as best he could, although he sure as hell didn't want to, Paulie stood and clapped his hands to get everyone's attention. Ben sat up behind him and wrapped his arms around Paulie's legs. Idly stroking Paulie's fuzzy thighs, which didn't help the reduction of Paulie's hard-on much, he rested his head at the side of Paulie's hip and watched the show unfold.

Paulie comfortably burrowed his hand into Ben's mop of hair while he spouted orders.

"Ben's moving in, guys. We need help unloading his truck. Why should my new lover and I do all the work when we have a pool full of goldbrickers lying around digesting my food even as their overworked livers process my liquor. You've been conscripted for the job. So don some clothes and let's hop to it."

"He must be joking," Jamie said to Trevor. "Clothes? What the hell are clothes?"

"Maybe he's mad from the heat," Trevor sighed, lying back with a yawn and draping an arm over his eyes to block out the sun. "Just ignore him."

"Otherwise the bar is closed forthwith!" Ben yelled, still snuggled up to Paulie's hip.

And suddenly Paulie's poolside was a whirlwind of activity.

"Where's my shirt?" Trevor cried, leaping to his feet.

"Pack a few drinks," Jamie whispered. "We'll take them with us."

"Massa's in a mood," Jeffrey cooed in Jack's ear. "Better lend a hand."

"I'd rather fuck," Jack answered, but he dragged himself out of the pool anyway.

"What, *again?*"

Danny stood by the diving board tugging on a pair of cutoffs, looking worried and cuter than hell. "Where's the truck? What do we do first? Do we have a dolly?"

Ben gazed up into Paulie's eyes. "Motivation." He grinned. "Works every time if you know which nerve to hit."

Paulie grinned back. "Apparently the human liver is *packed* with nerves, and you, my love, just hit every one of them."

Ben watched the gang scurrying about like rats, throwing on clothes, tucking in hard-ons. "Yeah," he said. "I guess I did."

BEN'S PIDDLING dab of furniture was absorbed inside the many rooms of Paulie's mansion and hardly left a ripple on the water. His Cannondale claimed a spot next to Paulie's Bianchi Campione road bike in the three-car garage alongside Paulie's surfboards and his grandmother's golf clubs and treadmill. His Audi station wagon filled the gap in the middle parking space of the garage while Paulie's Ford town car sat, as it always did, in the space nearest the house. For Ben's many books, Paulie allotted special shelves in the library Paulie's grandfather had built and his grandmother had so dearly loved. Ben's books, among Paulie's hundreds and his grandmother's thousands, hardly made a ripple either. For convenience sake, Ben's clothes were arranged on hangers in the walk-in closets of the bedroom adjoining Paulie's own, although Ben himself had not slept in that room since the second night of his visit.

The U-Haul truck was parked on the street until Ben could find time to drive it to the rental office, where it would be gladly dumped and abandoned like a mooching relative.

And with those chores done, Ben was home.

Dinner that night was a boisterous affair. Earlier, Paulie had stuffed an envelope filled with cash into Jeffrey's hand in appreciation for all he had done during the last two weeks, and Jeffrey had been so touched he'd scooped Paulie into his massive arms and squeezed him so tight Paulie thought he'd heard a tendon snap. Paulie told him not to serve dinner. Tonight his friends could damn well serve themselves. Jeffrey was no longer an employee. For their last night together, he had been promoted to full-fledged guest. Jeffrey was so touched by the gesture he scooped Paulie into his arms *again.* This time Ben caught them hugging in the hallway and, with a good-natured growl, dragged Paulie into his own arms instead. Everyone laughed.

In the formal dining room, Paulie sat at the head of the dinner table on his grandmother's needlepoint chair with Ben occupying the chair next to him. Jeffrey and Jack cuddled and whispered and giggled along the right side of the long mahogany table, and Jamie, Trevor, and Danny cuddled and whispered and giggled along the opposite side to his left. Hammer was perched on a stack of pillows in the chair at the foot of the table with a napkin tied around his neck and a foil party hat secured on top his head. Since he was being allowed full eating privileges, he deigned to leave the silly hat where it was for the time being, but as soon as the food ran dry, he planned to rip it to shreds. Hammer was pretty sure it made him look stupid.

Paulie stood and hoisted his wine glass. "To good friends," he said as Ben pulled himself to his feet and draped an arm around Paulie's waist, his wine glass also held aloft. A moment later everyone was standing and leaning in to clink glasses together, jabbering out their own little toasts and words of appreciation to their host, for which Paulie humbly bowed and said thank you very sweetly. Hammer barked and scooped up a dinner roll from Trevor's plate while no one was looking.

Before dinner was over, eight bottles of wine and six bottles of champagne had been consumed. And it wasn't cheap stuff either. Paulie was glad his friends would be leaving the next day. Two more weeks in their company and he would have to take out a mortgage on the mansion to pay down his tab at the Liquor Barn.

Jamie and Trevor cornered Paulie and Ben in the kitchen before everyone toddled off to bed. Their four-way hug lasted almost a minute.

Finally, with misty eyes, and slightly embarrassed by their sentimentality, they tore themselves from each other's grasp.

"It's been a hoot," Trevor said, sniffing and looking sad.

Jamie was *really* drunk. "Hootalicious," he said, dropping his head to Trevor's shoulder. Tears were streaming down his face. "We love you guys so much."

"We love you back." Ben grinned at Jamie. "And your fly's open."

"Good," Trevor said, slapping Jamie's hand away from the offending wardrobe malfunction. "That'll be one less thing to worry about when we get upstairs."

Trevor reached out and patted Paulie's cheek. Then he patted Ben's. To Ben, he said, "Paulie has been in love with you forever. We're glad you finally made him a happy man. And we're glad you finally discovered who you really are. Now you can be a happy man too."

Ben smiled, honestly touched. "Thank you."

Jamie seemed a little less touched. "Although the preacher must be shitting hymnals."

"Actually," Ben said, "he took the news remarkably well."

"You don't say," Trevor pondered, rather like Hercule Poirot exercising his little gray cells in pursuit of the solution to a particularly enticing conundrum.

"Oh, but I *do* say."

And as if he had forgotten to mention it, Ben turned to Paulie. "Funny thing. Pop's taken down that gigantic thermometer in front of the church."

Paulie looked a little uncomfortable all of a sudden. He resisted the urge to shuffle his feet and look guilty. "Well, what do you know?"

"Yeah, and he asked me to give you a message. He says to tell you you're going to heaven. Says he's not too sure about me, but he's pretty sure you've got an all-expense-paid one-way ticket waiting for you at the gate. Full comps for all eternity."

"Really?"

"Yes. He said St. Peter's holding it for your sorry ass."

"Your father said *that?*"

"Well, no. I'm paraphrasing."

Paulie turned back to Trevor and Jamie in hopes of changing the subject, but Ben took a firm grip on his chin and dragged his face back to him.

"Why are your ears red? They only do that when you're coming or when you're sick."

"I'm coming—no, wait. I have the flu."

Ben cocked his head to the side and narrowed his eyes. "Amazing. Two lies in one sentence."

To change the subject, Paulie said the first thing that came to mind. "I think your father's wrong. I think my chances of getting into heaven are pretty slim."

"So do I," Ben chirped.

"Then why do you suppose he would tell you something like that?" Paulie knew he shouldn't have asked that question the second the words were out of his mouth, but of course, by then it was too late.

Ben cast his eyes to the ceiling, then slowly lowered them, smiling benignly. "He said it had something to do with the church roof."

Paulie decided to shoot for a totally innocent expression. "How odd."

"Yes," Ben said. "And it gets odder. He said it also had something to do with a furnace and two thousand square feet of wood flooring."

Paulie jumped. "What? I promised him *carpet! Carpet!* And he told me it was only fifteen hundred square yards!"

Ben shrugged, biting back a grin. "Well, that's Pop. And he didn't say *he* was going to heaven. He said you were. Oh, and he also mentioned a new air conditioner would be nice."

"Tell him to fuck off."

Ben smiled. "You can tell him yourself. We're going to services Sunday morning. I promised him we would. He wants to introduce the church's benefactor to the congregation. You'll be a star. Thrilling, huh? He's even going to put your name on one of the pews. You'll be an *immortal* star with reserved seating every single Sunday."

Paulie didn't like the sound of that. "Every Sunday? I have to go to church *every Sunday?*"

Ben nodded. "Every fucking Sunday. Not only do you have to go, but he expects me to come with you. I'm not happy about this Paulie. I hate going to church."

Paulie groaned. "So do I." Suddenly he felt that boulder in his stomach again. Reverend Martin's sermons were *long.* And *boring.*

"Burning in hell would be easier," he mumbled.

"Tell me about it," Ben groused.

While Jamie and Trevor howled with laughter, Paulie took a fistful of Ben's shirt and dragged his face in close.

"But you still love me, right?"

Ben's eyes warmed. He scooped Paulie into his arms. "Yes. I still love you. My only worry now is that you'll go to heaven and I'll burn in hell."

Paulie nestled his face in Ben's neck. "Well, maybe if you play your cards right, I'll buy the air conditioner in your name. Then you can go to heaven too."

Ben thunked his head down on Paulie's chest. "Great. My father's an extortionist and my lover's a ready victim."

"You're worth it," Paulie cooed.

Trevor watched this interchange with proud patience. Then he decided he'd heard enough. He turned to Jamie. "Let's go fuck Danny."

Jamie perked right up. "Good idea. Unless I'm sorely mistaken, these two are about to get maudlin. I hate maudlin."

"Me too."

"Toodles," they said in unison.

And with that they were gone.

When they were alone, Paulie snuggled into Ben's welcoming arms. "Tell me you're not mad about me buying off your father by paying for the roof. Or the furnace. Or the fucking hardwood floor."

Ben smiled. "I'm not mad."

Paulie pulled him closer. "Will you be mad if I tell him the air conditioner is out of the question?"

Ben kissed the tip of Paulie's nose. "As long as you're the one to tell him, no. I won't be mad. Although I think he's already announced it."

"Great. Good thing I'm rich, huh?"

"You bet."

"Will you love me when I'm old and poor, Ben?"

"Yes, Paulie. I'll love you when you're old."

"You didn't mention poor."

"I'll get back to you on that one."

"You're your father's son."

"That hurt."

And arm in arm, they wandered off to bed, chuckling.

Tail high, and not quite sure what the hell was going on, Hammer trailed along behind.

JOHN INMAN has been writing fiction since he was old enough to hold a pencil. He and his partner live in beautiful San Diego, California. Together, they share a passion for theater, books, hiking and biking along the trails and canyons of San Diego or, if the mood strikes, simply kicking back with a beer and a movie. John's advice for anyone who wishes to be a writer? "Set time aside to write every day and do it. Don't be afraid to share what you've written. Feedback is important. When a rejection slip comes in, just tear it up and try again. Keep mailing stuff out. Keep writing and rewriting and then rewrite one more time. Every minute of the struggle is worth it in the end, so don't give up. Ever. Remember that publishers are a lot like lovers. Sometimes you have to look a long time to find the one that's right for you."

You can contact John at john492@att.net, on Facebook: http://www.facebook.com/john.inman.79, or on his website: http://www.johninmanauthor.com/.

Also from JOHN INMAN

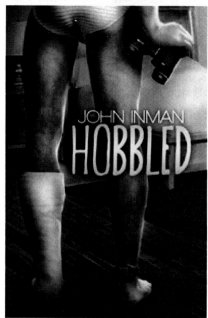
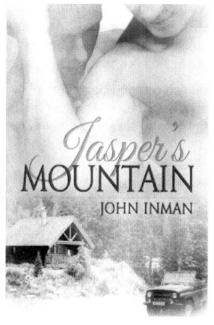

Also from JOHN INMAN

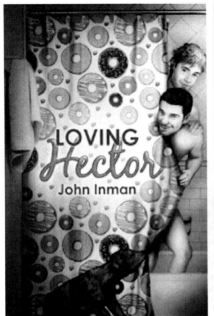

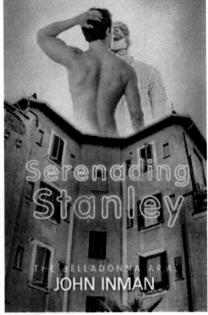

Also from JOHN INMAN

http://www.dreamspinnerpress.com

Also from DREAMSPINNER PRESS

On ARCHIMEDES STREET

Jefferson Parrish

http://www.dreamspinnerpress.com

Also from DREAMSPINNER PRESS

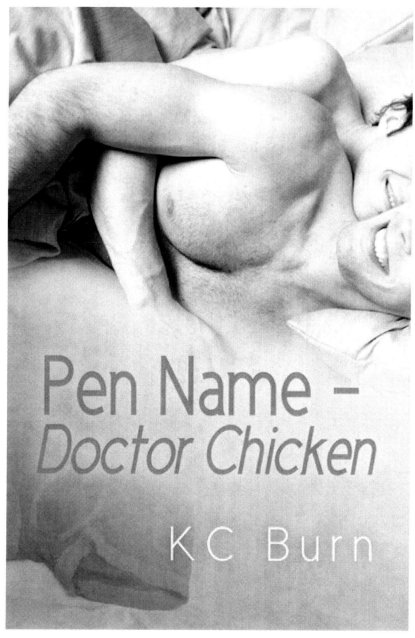

Pen Name –
Doctor Chicken

K C Burn

http://www.dreamspinnerpress.com

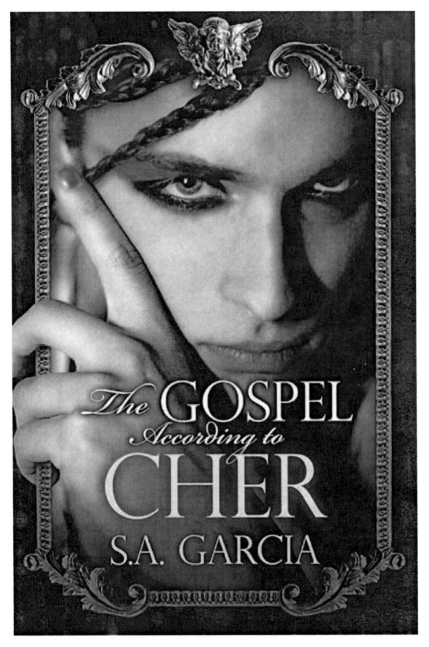

Also from DREAMSPINNER PRESS

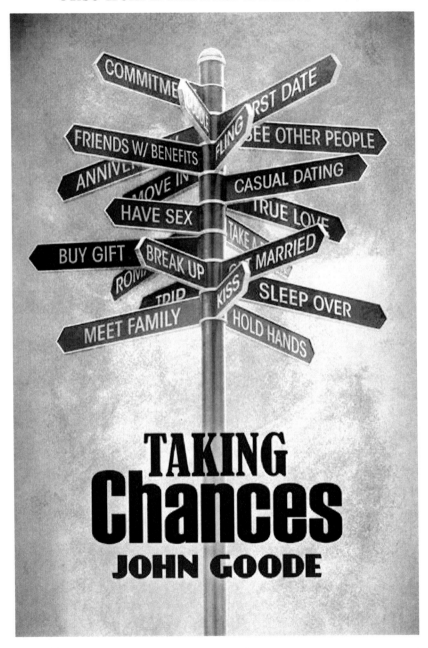

Also from DREAMSPINNER PRESS

http://www.dreamspinnerpress.com